SPECTRE AT THE FEAST
Book 3 of the East Berlin Series

Also by Max Hertzberg

The East Berlin Series
Stealing The Future (2015)
Thoughts Are Free (2016)
Spectre At The Feast (2017)

Other Fiction
Cold Island (2018)
Stasi Vice (2018)

Non-fiction
with Seeds For Change
How To Set Up A Workers' Co-op (2012)
A Consensus Handbook (2013)

After the experience of the East German political upheaval in 1989/90 Max Hertzberg became a Stasi files researcher. Since then, he has also been a book seller and a social change trainer and facilitator.

Visit the author's website for background information on the GDR, features on this series and its characters, as well as guides to walking tours around the East Berlin in which these books are set.

www.maxhertzberg.co.uk

SPECTRE AT THE FEAST
Book 3 of the East Berlin Series

Max Hertzberg

 WOLF PRESS

K 1.1 2 3 4 5 6 7 8 9 10

Published in 2017 by WOLF PRESS.
www.wolfpress.co.uk

Wolf Press, 22 Hartley Crescent, LS6 2LL

A CIP record for this title is available from the British Library
ISBN: 978-0-9933247-4-1 (paperback), 978-0-9933247-5-8 (epub)

Set in 10½ on 12pt Linux Libertine O and 11/16/24pt Linux Biolinium O
Printed by Amazon

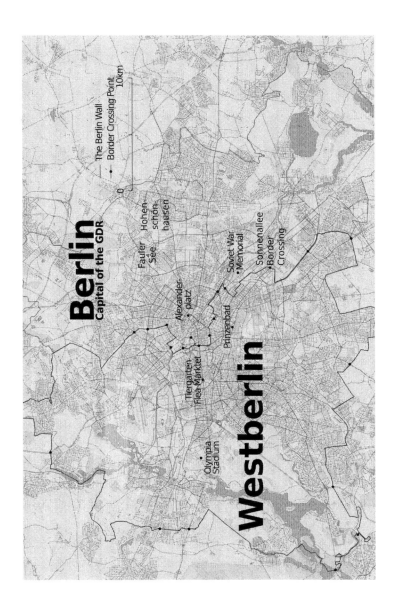

Berlin showing West Berlin and
Berlin, Capital of the GDR

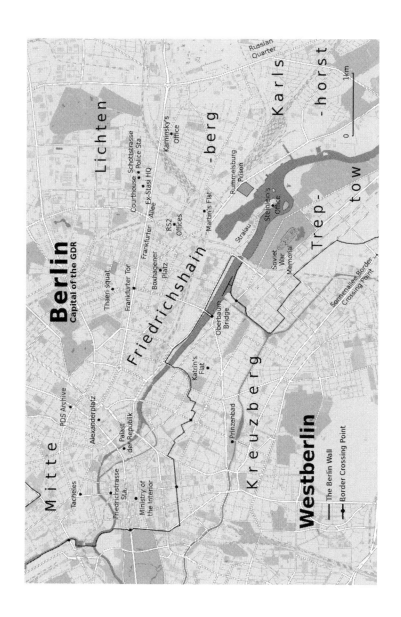

Central Berlin

PART 1
Democracy

Day 1
Sunday
12th June 1994

Kaminsky stood on scaffolding at the end of Alexanderplatz, one arm raised, fist clenched, saluting the crowds below. He stared out at thousands of faces, at hundreds of placards and banners, flags and flaming torches.

The crowd chanted. *Kaminsky Kaminsky Kaminsky.*

But Kaminsky stood above them all, stock still, fist raised, saying not a word.

The crowd hushed itself, the shouts and chants dying back, murmuring to a standstill.

Only when he had absolute silence did Kaminsky lower his arm and step up to the microphones and cameras.

The government is weak.

The government has lost its way.

They even held a referendum to ask us what to do, but they're still unsure: parliament and Round Tables are bickering.

Our government is paralysed.

But we, the people, we are making history. Right now, all of us here are making history.

And more than ever, in this historical time we need a capable leader. A leader to steer a steady course for our Republic. We need a leader with strength, a leader of ability and moral fibre. It is time to end the political corruption—but the establishment doesn't recognise this.

It is time to renew our democratic system—but the establishment won't do this.

It is time for real leadership—but the establishment can't provide this!

Again the chant *Kaminsky Kaminsky Kaminsky* swept through the crowd. Kaminsky himself stood back, let the wave of words break on the stage and surge around.

Look at the Resurgence: just a few weeks ago the government of this country was unable to deal with violence and criminality from skinheads and far-right extremists. The establishment showed itself unable to act.

We, the people, took matters into our own hands.

We, the people, cleared up the mess they couldn't handle.

We, the people, exposed the weakness of the elite!

It is time for us, the people, to take back control.

It is time for us, the people, to take back power.

Because we are the people!

Kaminsky stood back, his fist raised again, smiling and acknowledging the chants of the crowd.

We are the people! We are the people! We are the people!

20:13
Karo

I don't think anyone saw us.

My mate Schimmel was on the street corner, keeping a lookout while I decorated the window with red paint. I'd only got as far as RACIST SCUM before I was overcome by the sour taste of anger that rippled up my throat. *Fuck it.* With the heel of my boot I kicked a cobble loose and levered it out.

I took a few steps back, turned, and lobbed the stone.

The window of Kaminsky's office cracked, the glass hanging for a moment before sliding down, shattering as it went. Schimmel twisted around, shock splashed over his face. I grabbed his hand as I legged past him.

At the U-Bahn station we jumped down the steps as a train pulled in and I sat down, laughing at the dismay on my friend's coupon.

"That wasn't the deal!" he said.

"You feeling sorry for Kaminsky?"

Schimmel didn't answer, and I stopped grinning. It was no fun any more, not with my friend looking so pissed off all the time.

"Oh, come on." I tried again. "He deserves more than a smashed window!"

"He does. But what about sticking to agreements?"

"Fuck off!"

The train was pulling into the next station. As I stepped onto the platform my anger and frustration felt like a kick in the back.

20:46

Martin

The police lieutenant limped into my flat on a Sunday evening. He wasn't in uniform and I was just about naïve enough to assume this might be a social visit: *just passing, thought I'd pop in.*

"They let you out?" I asked as I held the door open.

"Had to argue with the surgeon." Steinlein's stick tapped over my painted floorboards.

I offered my visitor the comfy seat, but he preferred the hard kitchen chair at the table. I was about to offer him coffee too, but he lit a cigarette and started to speak.

"I know you're still on leave but I was hoping you could help me with a case. It's sensitive."

The shift in his voice warned me even before his words reached me. This was work. This was police work. I got up, carefully pushed my chair back under the table and stood by the door, pointing out into the hallway.

"You want a cup of coffee, you're welcome. But if you

3

want to get me involved in something ... You know why I'm still on leave? It's not because of this," I touched my bruised panda eyes, the eyebrows that were still growing back, "nor because of this," I pointed at my left knee. "They say it's because I need a rest." I tapped the side of my head. "I think I've had enough of *sensitive*, don't you, comrade Lieutenant?"

"When the fascists attacked me, when I was in hospital, you were the only one to come to visit." Steinlein was still sitting there, hands clasped over the top of his walking stick.

"Doesn't make me responsible for you."

"Think about it. Call me when you're ready to talk." Steinlein got to his feet, holding on to the table for support, then tapped his way back into the hall, as slowly as he'd come in. By the time he was at the door, curiosity had got the better of me.

A curiosity I thought long gone. A curiosity I should have known better than to allow myself.

"What is it? What's so bloody *sensitive*?"

With one hand on the latch Steinlein half turned to meet my gaze. "They want to kill Kaminsky."

DAY 2
Monday
13th June 1994

First of all, let me thank you for inviting me onto the programme this morning. I like the radio, yes, it's true, I also like speaking on the radio—I think it's a democratic medium. Everyone has a radio, it's a good way to get the people's message out.

This morning I want to talk about the Round Tables. As you know, I'm an elected member of the Volkskammer, so I get around the ministries a lot. I see a lot of messengers from the Round Tables. We're not talking about one or two, but scores of them. These Round Table lackeys make vexatious queries, and they expect our government ministers to take time to deal with them.

They behave as though they were part of our democratically elected government.

But the Round Tables aren't elected. They're not even mentioned in the constitution. They are lobbies. Lobbies for unelected and unelectable busybodies.

These Round Tables, these lobbies, they're interfering in the serious business of running the country.

And what about Hanna Krause, the chair of the Central Round Table? She claims she can solve the problems of our country. But how can she solve any problems if she spends all her time sitting in meetings?

Let's be clear: Hanna Krause and her absurd knitting circles can't even solve their own problems, never mind the country's.

Karo

First thing this morning I knocked on Schimmel's door. I needed to talk about last night, but I also I wanted to talk to someone about Kaminsky. Schimmel's cool, we've known each other for years, from way back before the revolution started in 1989. We've had loads of fun together, the pair of us opened up the *Thaeri*, our squat near Frankfurter Tor, and we've been living there ever since.

Schimmel was still in bed, I crouched down on the floor in front of him and tried out a smile.

"You were right, I should have kept to our plan."

Schimmel didn't respond, his face stayed blank.

"But you gotta admit, it was the right thing to do?"

Again no reaction from my friend. I swivelled around on my heels, and sat down on the floor, back resting against the side of the bed.

"Can I have the old Schimmel back?" I asked his room.

I looked over my shoulder, Schimmel still hadn't reacted.

"Sorry," I said, feeling useless. I'd been trying to make a joke, but … ach, what was with all the thinking? I'm no good at that. I turned around again, kneeling on the floor, my elbows on the bed, my face close to Schimmel's. "Look, Schimmel, what can I do? You can't let this Becker take over your life, you've got to deal with it. Come on, talk to me!"

In one quick movement Schimmel sat up, leaning against the wall, but still avoiding my eye. We both stayed like that for what seemed like ages, then in another quick movement he got up, pulling on jeans and a t-shirt.

"What can I do?" I asked him again.

Schimmel was buckling his belt, but he stopped, just long enough to shrug.

I felt like screaming at him, but instead I stood up, calmly as I could, and stood in front of him.

"Schimmel, I wasn't joking: I want my friend back. I want

the Schimmel I used to have. To get pissed with you, to dance to loud music with you. I want you to tell me boring shit about computers and to teach me how to pick locks and and and ... Whatever Becker did to you, we need to deal with it. I'm here, I want to help."

I got a nod for my efforts, but I wasn't complaining—right now that counted as progress.

"Can we talk about it?" I dunno, maybe I was pressing too hard, but it felt like I had to get Schimmel to talk. "How about tonight? We'll take some beers to the graveyard on Boxhagener Strasse. It's quiet there, nobody will bother us. We can have a chat."

Schimmel moved around me, heading towards the hall, but he stopped at the door. "Thanks, Karo," he said.

That was it. I didn't get a yes or a no. What was *Thanks* meant to mean?

After my pathetic attempts at getting through to Schimmel this morning I went to work. Sitting in the office and hassling people is nowhere near top of my list of things I like to do, in fact, it's not on the list at all. But that was my job today, and going by the reactions I was getting I reckon the people I was phoning didn't have me on their lists of good things either.

"It's Karo from RS2 in Berlin, I'm trying to get hold of someone from Antifa Weimar ... No I've been trying to get hold of someone, anyone, for the last week, is there no-one around? OK, yeah, please. No, no, don't phone me back! I'll wait. Just go and get her."

I doodled on the desk blotter as the person in Weimar went to see if they could find someone from the local Antifa group. Down the line I could hear loads of banging doors and heavy steps. Eventually the phone was picked up at the other end.

"Yeah?" said a voice.

"Who am I talking to?"

"Who's asking?" The voice didn't sound particularly suspicious, it was just routine.

"This is Karo from RS2 in Berlin-"

"Yeah, Bert told me about you. What do you want?" A bit warmer now, but still not like she was pleased to speak to me or anything.

For what felt like the millionth time today, I explained what I was trying to find out: whether local Antifa groups were working with the Round Tables on the accountability processes for the skinheads, how that was going etc etc et cete*fucking*ra.

"We haven't had much time for that kind of thing," the voice from Weimar said. "All the Thuringian fash and hools are working with Kaminsky's lot now. There's been loads of pro-Kaminsky demos and stuff like that, but whenever anyone objects the hools kick off, scaring off anyone who might say anything against Kaminsky. *Defending democracy* they're calling it. Basically we're just trying to protect counter-demos from Kaminsky's thugs. We're back to where we were before we all got together to kick the skinheads out. It's pretty scary; we could really do with a hand down here."

"It's happening everywhere and we've got to do something about it!"

They were so lame, I could predict exactly how they would react. Klaus, smoking his foul cigar and chewing on his sad moustache; Erika, keeping shtumm while she thought things through; and Laura—don't get me started on Laura, tutting and giving me her disapproving looks. Grit was there too, but she never says anything, she's *just* the secretary. What a group, what a hierarchy!

"Karo, you know how things stand," Laura began the inevitable lecture. "The *Republikschutz* is being wound up. We have one final job, and that is our only concern right now."

Blah blah blah, I thought viciously, trying not to say anything out loud. She was right, she was always right, but it was just the way she said things: she ate five lemons every morning for breakfast, I was dead sure of it.

Our only concern (according to Laura) was to co-ordinate the debriefing of skinheads and fascists. A lot of them were wanting to turn over a new leaf right now, all dead keen to prove how socially acceptable they were after they got their collective arse kicked during the Resurgence last March. That was absolutely ace, the way people just walked out of work and ganged up on the skins. But now we were dealing with the bureaucratic aftermath. Basically, for us, said Laura, that meant lots of phone calls and boring meetings with committees like the Commission for Truth and Reconciliation.

Except that's not what it was like any more. It had all changed sometime last week, maybe even the week before. All of a sudden the skins weren't that keen to be accepted back into society, they were more interested in playing bovva boys for Kaminsky and his mates.

The room had gone quiet and I realised that Laura had finished. Everyone was looking at me, waiting for a response.

"But he's dangerous!" I didn't know what response was expected, but I knew what I had to say about the situation. "We can't just ignore him! Kaminsky is out to destroy everything we've achieved since 1989! The way he's blocking the constitutional amendment on the Round Tables—he's threatening the Round Tables, and he's got that sick fixation on Hanna Krause, it's dead creepy. And then there's the fash; he's supporting the fash, they're doing their thing again-"

"Karo." This time it was Erika, I like Erika, so I let her interrupt me. "I don't think anyone disagrees with you. But we can't do anything about it. We can't take on any new cases, we don't have the mandate any more. It's a job for the police now."

I snorted but didn't say anything, just kept my eyes fixed on the papers in front of me, letting the meeting drone on around me.

I was still sitting there, arms crossed over my chest, staring at the desk in front of me when Erika touched my shoulder. Everyone else had left, the meeting must have ended, just me and Erika in the room.

She sat down next to me, doing that thinking thing she always does.

"Kaminsky worries me," she said after a while. She was still frowning, still deep in thought. "He's finding ways to tap into people's fears, promising them security at a time when there isn't any to be had. He's creating scapegoats, directing people's fear and anger."

"Like Hanna Krause? OK, I get it that he doesn't like the Round Tables, but does he have to personally attack the chair of the Central Round Table? The way he objectifies her, the other day he called her a *prattling woman* ..."

"I've known Hanna Krause for years, she's strong, she can take it."

"It's not about whether she can take it—she shouldn't have to!"

"We put up with far worse in the past. But you're right, she shouldn't have to put up with Kaminsky's slurs, and I don't know why she does. I reckon she knows what she's doing, she's probably got some plan up her sleeve."

There wasn't much to say to that.

"I went to one of his rallies," Erika continued. I looked up in surprise and she nodded. "I was curious to see his appeal-"

"How could you? Kaminsky is scum! A racist, sexist, nationalist bigot!" Erika nodded again, but I'd only just started my rant. "And we have to do something-"

"Yes, yes. You said that before, and we agree with you. But the *Republikschutz* isn't the right organ for that task. Look,

Martin always said we were stronger when we acted as individuals. He felt that his work at RS was too bound up in rules, regulations, protocol. He felt like it tied his hands and made him unable to act. Whereas when we act in our capacity as responsible citizens ..."

"You think we should keep an eye on Kaminsky, but not in any kind of official way?"

"Somebody needs to do it. And if it can't be RS ..."

Erika was right, RS wasn't the right tool for this job. I'd have to take my concerns elsewhere.

15:27
Karo

I left early that day. It didn't count as bunking off because I don't have fixed hours at the *Republikschutz*—I'm just helping out while Martin's on sick leave. But it felt like I was sneaking out, and Grit gave me a wink as I edged out of the office.

As soon as I got home I checked whether Schimmel was in, and, to be honest, I was a bit relieved when I couldn't find him. The usual aceness of living with Schimmel had turned into something else, in fact it kind of felt like I was living with his ghost. It started back in March: we were on a demo when he just lost it. He saw a face from the past, from when he was in the borstal or something, and it made him seriously flip. Knowing why he's changed doesn't really help though—like last night, just a simple change of plan and he totally freaks out on me. It's hard to deal with.

So I went to see Antifa Bert. It's not like he's number 2 on my list or anything, it's just I knew where to find him: sitting in the back bar of the *Schreina*.

"Anything going on?" I nodded towards the CB that Bert was monitoring just in case any alarm calls from other squats and social centres came in.

"Nah, been quiet since the Resurgence. I reckon we can

get rid of all this tat."

"Rumours are, the skins have started supporting Kaminsky."

"Re-educating them, isn't he? Doing a good job too, from what I hear." Bert fiddled with the CB kit for a bit, ignoring me while I did a sceptical face. But then he must have felt the need to justify what he'd just said. "Kaminsky's a socialist, he's got nothing in common with the fash."

"Yeah, but the way he goes on about *common sense* and stuff like that, that we need to use common sense when it comes to deciding who we let into our country, he goes on about needing to control immigration—that kind of stuff, it's all a bit-"

"Give the man a break! He's casting his net wide, trying to get people involved. It'll all come together."

Now Bert was in a huff. I hadn't expected this, but I knew what he was like when he was in a mood. There was no point trying to talk to him right now. Probably hungover or something.

16:39
Karo

I still felt the need to talk to someone about Kaminsky (and I guess about Schimmel too) but wasn't sure who. Normally I'd talk to Martin but it didn't feel fair to pile all this stuff on him when he was on sick leave.

So I decided to talk to his daughter, Katrin. I'd only known her since last autumn, same as Martin, but I really liked both of them. Martin could be hard work but Katrin and I got along really well, and it felt like we'd got close back in March when the fash were targeting her dad and the shit was really hitting the fan. We'd seen each other a lot back then, but not so much lately—too busy with work. Now I was in West Berlin, ringing her doorbell, hoping she'd be in.

Katrin opened the door, and when she saw me on the

stairs she gave me a lovely big smile and opened her arms for a hug. That felt good, just what I needed after the last few days.

"You got time for a visitor?"

"For you, always. Come in, I've got cake."

I followed her into the kitchen, and helped myself to a bottle of *Apfelschorle* from her fridge.

"Just as bad here as where I've come from," I nodded towards the kitchen table.

Pieces of paper were everywhere, and a tiny tape recorder lay on top. I picked it up—it was a bit longer than my hand, thick as a well-made sandwich. I was going to try out the buttons but Katrin took it off me.

"Don't—you'll lose my place. I've got to transcribe all these interviews for my dissertation, it's so boring, people just say the most banal things."

"I know all about people talking shite, at least I don't have to write it all down!"

Katrin smiled, but I didn't want the conversation to head towards work so I changed tack. "What you listening to?" It was something poppy, but kind of nice too. The singer had a terrific voice.

"Everything But The Girl, new album came out today. Do you want me to change it? Something heavier?" Katrin had given me the tea pot and two mugs, and was carrying a couple of slices of *Linzer Torte* into the living room.

I told her the music was fine and we sat together on the couch. It was nice and cool in her flat, she had the windows closed and the curtains drawn, keeping the heat out. It was cosy.

We talked a bit, and I told her about Schimmel, and she listened. She was a good listener, didn't interrupt, just sat there and paid attention. After a while I'd said everything there was to say.

"What about you?" she asked.

I gave her a whaddyatalkingabout face.

"Well it can't be easy on you either, seeing your friend like that."

"I'm fine."

"You're fine?" Katrin laughed at me. "You say me and my dad clam up when it comes to talking about feelings but you're just as bad!"

I slouched down a bit further on the sofa and crossed my arms.

"Karo, I'm just trying to help. I'm sorry I laughed at you."

I ignored her for a moment or two, but couldn't ignore the fact that she was right—this whole thing about Schimmel was stressing me out.

"It's like I can't get through to him. I'm beating myself up about it because it feels like I'm not doing enough, or not doing the right things. And that hurts. We've known each other for years, Schimmel and me. He's my best friend, he was my first proper friend. Now all of a sudden it's like he's not there any more. It used to be so good, we got up to all kinds of stuff, we put up with loads of hassle from the cops and the Stasi but we never let it get us down."

"Was it bad for you, back then?"

"Just the usual." I thought back to a few years ago, when the *Volkspolizei* would patrol Berlin, looking for punks to hassle. *We'll have to ask you to accompany us to the station. We need to verify your identity.* Like ten times a week, more if there was some state celebration coming up. They'd beat us up on Alex, or on the way home, pretty much all the time. "Just constant harassment. It's not like we'd ever have admitted it but I guess it did wear us down." God, I was glad those days were over! "What about you?"

"Wasn't too bad. The thing I'll never forgive them for is the way they made me leave school at 16. I really wanted to go to university, but there was never any chance of that happening."

"Was that why you left the country?"

"No." Katrin hesitated, her eyes fixed on the cup of tea between her hands. "They asked me to spy on my dad. That was the last straw, that's when I knew I had to get out. So we went to Hungary, me and this boy. We got out that way. I'll never forget the date: twenty-seventh of September 1989."

"Did you tell Martin? About what the Stasi asked you to do?"

"I should have done, I should have shouted it from the rooftops. I know that now, but I didn't then. I left instead. Hardest thing I've ever done."

I put my hand over Katrin's.

"Thing is, those same bastards are still around." I could hear the tension in Katrin's voice, winding itself up, tighter and tighter. "And it's like they've still got it in for my dad. That thing with Evelyn last year, and you can bet they were behind the fascist stuff in spring. They're definitely helping Kaminsky, right now. They're never going to give up, not until they're back in power. Will we never get rid of them?"

"Is that why you're still in the West?"

Katrin lifted her cup of tea to her lips, shaking my hand off. She sipped, then lowered the cup again.

"There's no way I can be in the same country as those Stasi bastards."

"What do you know about this Becker guy?" After a long silence Katrin had started talking about Schimmel again. "Are you sure he's responsible for how Schimmel is now?"

I didn't know the answer to that. Wish I did. I told Katrin I was going to find that out: along with who he was, what he'd done, where to find him.

"Is that wise? You might rake up more than Schimmel can handle."

I thought about that for a while, but it was obvious that the only way to go was through Becker, and it was already weeks and weeks ago that I'd promised myself that I'd find that man and do bad things to him. I mean, it was the whole reason I'd agreed to work with RS in the first place, I thought being in the *Republikschutz* would help me find him. But I'd been sidetracked into meetings and other stuff like all this shit around Kaminsky. I'd lost sight of my main mission.

So it was time to stop saying I was going to track that bastard down and actually start doing it. Talking with Katrin had helped me see that I really, really needed to get my shit together. I needed to get on Becker's case.

"Katrin, I've gotta go, I'm meant to be meeting up with Schimmel. Look, thanks for the chat." I gave her a peck on the cheek. "I'm glad we talked. It helped."

"Do you want to come round sometime, dinner maybe?"

"Dinner? Ooh, how bourgeois!" But then I saw Katrin's face, and that made me shut my stupid gob. "I mean, yeah, sounds great. Tell you what, I'll bring you a tape—broaden your musical horizons a bit!"

22:20

Karo

I was a bit surprised, but actually really glad that Schimmel was up for that chat I'd suggested. It was getting late and the streets were quiet. It was still hot but it felt a bit fresher under the trees in the graveyard. We found a bench at the back where no-one was going to bother us or look all shocked just because we had a few drinks with us.

I opened the beers and handed one to Schimmel, then tapped my own bottle against his. "*Prosit*".

We sat there for a while not saying much. I'd already thought about how to play this and I'd decided I was going to have to take it slow and be dead patient. That was fine, we had enough beer for a long sesh.

But Schimmel didn't look like he was going to say anything. So I decided to kick it off: "Do you want to talk about it?"

Schimmel shook his head. *Great start, well done Karo.*

"OK, I'll start talking, yeah? Look, the way I see it, everything was fine until that demo in March. You saw this guy Becker, he was hanging out with the Nazis, and you flipped out and haven't been the same since." Schimmel hadn't objected so far, so I carried on. "Is Becker from the borstal? The one they put you in back in '88? Did something happen?"

Schimmel shook his head again. I took a pull of my beer, giving him time to say something.

"Not the borstal. He was the boss at the *Durchgangsheim*." The temporary secure unit for juvenile delinquents.

Schimmel hadn't touched his beer yet.

"The night we met, at the Erlöser Church, was that the day they let you out?" Still no reaction from Schimmel. "You know, I thought you were really sorted."

I got half a grin for that and Schimmel finally lifted the bottle to his lips. "Really? I was well fucked. Didn't know whether to be happy I was free or scared because I had the Stasi on my back, trying to recruit me."

"You did the right thing."

"I was shitting myself."

We smiled at that. Memories. It had been a good day when I met Schimmel, I was glad we'd met. Schimmel was necking his beer, letting the alcohol flow down his throat without swallowing. He was working up to something.

"I was thirteen when they put me in the hard room," he said finally. "I must have been about 43 when they let me out." He'd pulled his knees up into his chest and was staring at the ground.

"What's the hard room?" I asked.

Schimmel shook his head. "On the first day I didn't get any food. After that I got dry bread and thin soup." He was still talking to his knees, the beer bottle held loosely in one

17

hand. "The bread was so hard that I had to put it in the soup. It soaked up all the liquid and all I had left was bread," his words were coming in spurts and stammers. But I didn't push, I just waited, let him talk in his own time, to the rhythm of his memories.

"There was no window in the room, not even a bulb. In the evening they opened the door and I was blinded by the light from outside. They put down a bowl of soup and threw the bread on the floor. There'd be two of them, the other one used to throw a smelly mattress in and then they closed the door on me."

I sat there, next to Schimmel, not knowing what to say, what to do. I wanted to put my arms around him, but was frightened he would stop talking. All this time and he'd never said anything about this. Nothing at all.

"One day, when they threw the mattress at me, it landed on top of the bowl. The soup spilt over the floor. They just laughed, said it served me right for being careless. I tried to lick the soup off the floorboards, but it had soaked into the dust and between the cracks. I cried for hours. I cried until the morning when they took the mattress and the bowl away."

I couldn't hold back any more, this was my friend. I put my arms round him. He was shivering.

"So what are we going to do?" I asked after a while, but Schimmel had gone quiet again. All this pain, this State had fucked up so many of us. And the people who had done this to us, they had names and addresses. "Schimmel, we can't let them get away with this," I was trying to tread carefully, unsure how to say what I was thinking. "If you tell me what you know about Becker, I'll track him down. It should be dead easy for me to do that, now I'm working at RS-"

But it was the wrong thing to say, Schimmel just closed down again. In fact, he put the bottle of beer on the floor, dead carefully, just by his feet. Then he stood up and walked away.

"Schimmel!"

He didn't turn around, but I think he said: *It's my problem,* something like that.

"Schimmel!"

But he'd gone, he was already round the corner, behind the trees.

"Fucking Becker!" I threw my bottle at a headstone. "What did you do to my mate, you shit!" The bottle smashed as it hit, beer spraying over the granite. It made a good noise but didn't make me feel any better.

DAY 3
Tuesday
14th June 1994

We value those who have come to the GDR. We value those who contribute to our economy and our society. But the crucial issue is that it has to be the government that makes decisions about people coming in.

That is a difference between what I stand for and what the Round Tables want. It is very simple, when I look at the issues facing us, I consider the issue, I set out my plan, and I stick to it. It's called leadership.

Hanna Krause and her talking shops can't provide leadership. Only a strong government provides leadership.

We need a strong government—a strong government will give us steady employment. A strong government will give us consumer goods. And a strong government will give us back the respect of the world that we deserve.

08:05
Karo

"Erika, I'm quitting."

I'd thought about it a lot, and it was definitely the right thing to do. Talking to Katrin had made me think about it, and the scene last night in the graveyard had just confirmed my decision. I felt a bit bad about it though, Erika had asked me to help out at RS, and even though it was dead boring I guess the work I was doing was important.

"When?" asked Erika.

OK, I wasn't expecting wailing and gnashing of teeth, but Erika's reaction was a bit disappointing.

"Thanks a bunch, there was me thinking I'd been making myself indispensable."

I must have looked miserable because Erika put her arms around me. She had coffee breath but I didn't shy away; she was being nice.

"You are. You're doing brilliant liaison work with the Antifa groups around the country—that's the kind of thing we really need help with." She saw me rolling my eyes and responded: "It's true! But it's obvious you're not happy here, nor with the way we work."

"Thing is," what Erika had just said made me feel warm, it was good to get compliments—but I also had a favour to ask. "I want to quit, but I don't. See what I mean?"

Erika pulled her confused face. Which is kind of like her normal face, but I knew how to tell the difference by now.

"Remember when you offered me this job and I said I had a mission, and being in RS would help with that?" I still wasn't sure whether I should tell Erika this, but decided to go for it anyway. "A friend of mine, he was in borstal. Back before 1989. And he was in the *Durchgangsheim* here in Berlin. Something happened to him. *Someone* happened to him. Whatever it was, it wasn't nice. It was a member of staff —I'm going to track him down, make sure he pays for what he's done."

"What are you going to do?"

"That's up to my friend. I'm just here to find the man."

Erika had a good think about that, and I left her in peace while she got it all straight in her head.

"One of the staff? Party member?"

"Must have been. And it looks like he got involved in the

21

fascist scene, after '89."

"But if you quit your job here …"

"I won't have my RS identification any more, and I won't be able to access all the archives and records and stuff. So I'm thinking, I could quit, but not tell anyone. I'll just do this one thing then I'll quit officially, hand in my ID-"

"Karo, that's not the way it works." Erika didn't sound too pleased. "Let's talk to the others-"

"No way! There's no way Laura is going to let me do that kind of moonlighting, and Klaus isn't going to agree to it either!"

Somehow Erika persuaded me to take it to the meeting. It was my own fault, I shouldn't have mentioned it to her. But here I was, trying to explain to Laura and Klaus what I wanted. Grit was there too, but as usual she wasn't saying anything, just taking notes. Except she wasn't even doing that because I'd asked for this bit to be off the record.

"Highly irregular, young lady," said Laura, pretty much as I'd expected her to, but then she totally veered off-course. "What are you going to do with this man when you find him?"

I hesitated, I wanted to beat the shit out of him. But that wasn't really my decision, it was up to Schimmel.

"If this person were to be part of a restorative justice process then I'd have no objections to your trying to find him on work time," Laura continued.

I had to think about that. Could I give any guarantees? But before I had a chance to make any promises Klaus had decided it was his turn.

"You say this man you're trying to find was involved in the fascist scene? At decision-making level?" he tapped an unlit cigar on the tabletop for a moment or two, maybe he was giving me a chance to answer, but once again, before I could say anything he jumped in. "If it is the case that this

Becker fellow is a cadre-level Nazi then personally I'd regard the task of finding him and bringing him to justice as being within Karo's remit here at RS."

OK, this wasn't what I'd been expecting. I looked at my colleagues. Laura still had her beady eye on me while Klaus was chewing his cigar and looking up at the ceiling. Erika gave me a wink, and I had to try really hard not to giggle. But this was good, this was totally good. Basically I just had to agree not to beat Becker up. Or let anyone else do it. Still wasn't sure about that bit, but probably best to keep quiet for the moment.

"Shall we say two weeks? We can review the decision then," said Laura, still super-serious, but somehow looking a bit more human. Klaus just carried on chewing his cigar.

I looked around the table, I had the go-ahead from everyone.

Except Grit. Nobody ever asked the secretary what she thought. I don't know why I did, I mean it could have gone badly, she might have disagreed. But I asked her anyway.

"I think you should go for it," she said.

10:14
Martin

When Karo rang the doorbell I was sitting in my favourite chair, smoking a cigarette and thinking about Steinlein. The Jonathan Blues Band were in the background, playing *Little Peter*.

"Where have you been hiding?" she asked as she stomped into my flat.

"Speak for yourself."

"Yeah, sorry, Martin, been really busy. But you could at least pretend to be pleased to see me!"

"Coffee?" I offered, but Karo was already in the kitchen, filling a glass from the tap. As she gulped the water down I headed back to my chair.

Now Karo was poking around the kitchen. "Got any beer?" She was counting the empties behind the door.

"In the fridge. Bring me one too."

Karo came back into the living room, opening the bottle with her teeth

"Are you OK, Marty?"

"Why?"

"You always have a go at me when I take the top off with my teeth. Some remark about cracking them or chipping the enamel. You're smoking a cigarette even though you supposedly gave up last year. Plus it's not even midday and you're having a beer with me. See why I'm worried?"

I took a bottle off her and looked out the window. Maybe it had been a mistake to let Karo in, sometimes it took a lot of energy just to have a basic conversation with her.

"This is the bit where you tell me I shouldn't be worried."

Instead of answering her I clinked my bottle against hers, *Prosit!*

"What's on your mind?"

"Are you going to stop hassling me or do I have to throw you out?"

Karo slumped down in the chair opposite me, all the energy suddenly draining out of her. "Hassling mates into spilling their guts is becoming a habit. Sorry."

"RS?" I guessed.

Karo hesitated, working out whether I could deal with whatever she might say, then she blurted it all out anyway: "It sucks. It's like, I thought I could be doing something useful there, but you just get, like literally, trapped by this lurking *bureauctopus.*"

Her neologism made me laugh, and I got a cautious smile in return. "Drowning in paperwork?" I asked her.

She picked at the label on her beer bottle for a beat or two, then: "You going to tell me what's happening in your world?"

24

It was an obvious subject-changer, but I let her have it.

"Haven't you heard? I'm on sick leave."

"Yes." She gave me an exaggerated sigh that she probably thought suitably ironic. "I did hear something about that. But what are you doing—and please don't tell me you're sitting around all day listening to depressing '70s music and smoking like a Russian panzer!"

"Oh, I'm keeping busy."

"Martin, I'm going to be straight up with you because you're a mate: you look like shit. I mean, look out the window—the sun's blazing down, has been for weeks. Everyone's got sunburn. But you? You look like you've been living in Siberia."

"Been doing a bit of thinking."

"Kaminsky? Yeah, call me psychic if you want but that arsehole is on everyone's minds." She paused for a moment, then: "You're not going all Hamlet on me are you?" She looked pleased at her cultural reference.

"Who'd be my Ophelia?"

Karo looked blank for a moment, then a smile creased her face. "She's the one who went and drowned herself? Couldn't take any more of Hamlet being a misery-guts?"

Things lightened up a bit after that and we managed to get a bit of a conversation going. We talked about Kaminsky, and I suggested he was more Macbeth than Hamlet, but Karo didn't get the comparison.

"It's the whole referendum thing." I mashed out my cigarette. "People voted to wind up RS—that doesn't bother me, that's what I voted for, too. But the vote on the Wall, the way it's split straight down the middle—how can we move on from that?"

"Yeah, but people also voted to give the Round Tables some proper power," Karo said, still trying to cheer me up.

"Kaminsky and his party are blocking that. He just turned up, came out of nowhere." I replied. "As a country we were dealing with the problems, we got to grips with the skinheads and hooligans, but then we get Kaminsky, putting the brakes on devolution. He's like a ghost from the past: centralisation, crude nationalism, casual racism. It's like we've learned nothing, we're back to square one."

Karo had gone silent, as if talking about this stuff bored her. Except I knew it didn't. I knew she was as worried about all of this as I was.

"We're lacking passion." I told her, knowing I was going on a bit but unable to stop. "In the old days the Party gave us passion: love of the fatherland, a quasi-religious belief in Marxism-Leninism. But now we just appeal to people's rationality. It's not enough." I lit another cigarette, wondering where my words were taking me. "Where are the flags to identify with? Why aren't we celebrating what we've achieved? We don't do any of that. We just talk. We talk in meetings at work, we come home and have more meetings with the residents of our block. Then we go to our local Round Tables and talk some more. Talk, talk, talk. No passion. What kind of revolution is this with no singing and dancing? Is it any wonder so many are falling for Kaminsky's spectacle?"

"Shit, Martin, I was meant to be cheering you up and I've just got you all wound up about Kaminsky instead."

"I was already wound up before you came. But being pissed off isn't going to change anything. Never has."

11:55
Martin

Lieutenant Steinlein had found himself an office far from the curtain twitchers at his police station: a small set of buildings sat right at the end of the Stralau peninsular, beyond the cemetery and opposite the last boatyard. The oxidised sign on the gate said *Transport Pool of the Council of Ministers of the GDR,* but Steinlein hadn't been able to find any record of the property in the Council's records. He'd finally gone to the archives at the old Stasi HQ, and found it in a file covered by four years' worth of dust. Like so many others, this building had been forgotten.

"It was used by the Stasi. From here they kept an eye on the barge traffic heading to West Berlin," he said as he struggled with the lock.

The key finally turned and Steinlein pushed the door open. Stale heat escaped from the building, making me feel woozy. I regretted the beer I'd shared with Karo earlier.

I peered into the building, four years' worth of dust coated every surface here too.

"Those prints are mine." Steinlein pointed to the footprints tracking through the grime and mouse droppings. "I've been here a few times."

We went through a hallway, empty except for a dented weapons safe, the doors hanging open and the racks empty. A cardboard box sat on the shelf and I picked it up, tipping a long, slender bullet onto my palm. I turned the brass casing between my fingers, thinking how lucky we'd been in 1989— if it hadn't been for Gorbachev our revolution would have ended in a bloodbath.

I dropped the bullet into the box and put it back on the shelf. Steinlein watched me, his face without expression.

"I've been using one of the rooms upstairs," he said, limping towards the staircase.

I watched him edge up the stairs, favouring his left leg. When I'd first met him, during a police raid on a fascist squat, he'd been insouciant, almost to the point of insubordination. Now his earlier insolence had been replaced by a sober determination. I followed him to the first floor and into a room adorned with framed portraits of Honecker and Mielke. A big window overlooked the river, I could see from the Island of Youth right up to the *Weisse Flotte* moorings near the S-Bahn station. A dozen barges rested against pilings directly in front of us. It was a good view. Calming.

I opened a window, hoping to let out some of the heat and dust. Outside, the trees of Treptower Park were reflected in the slow flow of the river. The slight breeze came into the room, stirring dust.

"There are more desks and chairs in the other rooms, we'll set you up with somewhere to work from."

His attitude irritated me, I didn't like him assuming I'd do the job.

Grey archive boxes were stacked on the floor next to the window and files were spread across the table's surface. Steinlein shifted through the paperwork until he found what he wanted: an ordinary file, light coloured cardboard, a classification code pencilled on the front.

"Doctor Karl Kaminsky, recently elected to the Executive Committee of the PDS, the successor of the Communist SED party. Currently causing so much unrest in our Republic."

I took the cadre file and sat down.

"If you want my help you'll have to be completely open with me," I told him. It sounded trite but I was tired of being taken for a ride by members and ex-members of the security apparatus. "Why do you need my help, and why have you brought all these files here?"

Steinlein brushed his hair from his forehead, fixing his eyes on the portrait of Mielke hanging on the wall.

"Based on available intelligence and taking account of further political-operational indications that have been gained from operationally relevant contacts, we may anticipate that plans are being made to assassinate Kaminsky-"

"Why me? Why work from here and not the police station?"

"Operational information has been received from an individual with habitual residence in the Operational Area," Steinlein continued without pausing, ignoring my questions.

"I don't want a bloody report—just tell me what the hell is going on!"

Silence for a few seconds, then Steinlein exhaled, his back loosened and he turned to face me.

"There's a plot to kill Kaminsky, and I think police officers may be involved. I don't know who to trust, that's why I came to you. Will you help?"

"Make me a coffee, will you?"

I poked through the files while Steinlein boiled water on an electric plate. What the police lieutenant had said was serious, beyond serious. But I really didn't want to know, I'd done my bit, so many times, so many years. Doing my bit had broken me. Steinlein would have to find someone else to help him.

"I can't help," I called over to the policeman.

Steinlein measured out coffee grounds and poured boiling water into mugs. He limped back to the table with a mug in each hand, taking care not to spill any of the hot liquid.

"I know," he said when he got to the table. He put the mugs down. "But I don't know who else to trust. There's only you."

"How do you know whether you can trust me? Frankly, only a fool would." I got up, leaving the coffee on the table.

"Comrade Captain Grobe, when I was in hospital, you visited me and-"

"That's what you said the other day. So what, we were both beaten up by skinheads—doesn't make us best friends." I was already halfway to the door, keen to get out of this dusty sauna before I changed my mind.

"You impressed Neumann." Steinlein's superior officer, a hard-case in the political police department, K1.

"Neumann doesn't impress me," I called back.

"You've never been in the Party. You're capable. You have the necessary rank to lead this investigation. And you're not on active duty. No-one else fits the criteria." Steinlein stood up, facing me, his eyes trying to catch mine. "But most of all: you care. You care about our Republic. You care about what's happening to the GDR. And if you just stop for a moment, if you think for a moment, you'll know that right now the country is teetering on the edge—the referenda in April exposed the splits in our Republic. You know that if Kaminsky is assassinated then the whole country will tear itself apart."

Steinlein sat down again. "Think about it then tell me again that you won't help."

We stared at each other. He seemed to think he'd said enough, that I was a hungry fish ready to bite.

"You know something?" I broke the silence. "My shrink, I've only seen her once, but she says one of my symptoms is a lack of trust. She says I need to trust more. But I'm finding it hard to trust you right now. So will you cut the woffle and tell me why we're still talking?"

"You want it straight? Read this. It's not official, you'll see why. I haven't opened the usual criminal proceedings files because it's just been me working at this—read it, you'll see for yourself."

He gave me the folder he'd searched out before. The first sheet was an index of contents, usual stuff. The second sheet was an Information Report. Steinlein had detailed the steps leading up to this meeting. There weren't many, and they weren't convincing. It all boiled down to an anonymous tip-off: Kaminsky's life was in danger. Collateral material: zilch.

I shut the file and looked at Steinlein. He stared straight back, not even blinking.

"It's not much to go on, I know. But in the past I've had tip-offs from a source, good tip-offs. I think this is from the same person. On Saturday I took a delivery: internal Party documents. It was this new source, proving their value. I've been able to compare the material to some internal Situation and Development Reports. It all checks out." Steinlein was still staring at me, talking rapidly. "The Party has done some assessments for just this scenario; the Party actually believes an assassination attempt may happen."

"Fine, pass it on to the police, let K1 handle it—this is a political case."

"I had hoped someone with your background would understand—K1 is still too close to the Party. Before 1990 every single officer in K1 was a loyal member."

I must have looked confused, because Steinlein had to spell it out: "It's an internal threat. Someone or some faction within the Party wants to kill their own General Secretary."

12:03
Karo

It was totally out of order, the way the Party were hanging on to all these massive buildings. If it had been up to me they'd all be squats by now. Or theatres. Something like that anyway. I stood on the corner of Wilhelm-Pieck-Strasse and Prenzlauer Allee and looked up at the imposing columns that flanked the doors of *Haus der Einheit*. It looked dead posh, even with all the rendering falling off and the hardboard covering the broken windows.

I went into the lobby, it was all marble and big staircases, meant to make you feel that small. But it didn't work on me. Well, only a bit, and I made sure it didn't show. I spent a bit of time trying to work out which floor the archive was on, but all I could see on the big board at the bottom of the stairs was something called *Verbundarchiv*, and that didn't sound right.

"Can I help you, miss?" said a chalky voice.

It was some Party lackey, wearing a brown dust coat over his faded suit. But it wasn't that that bothered me, it was the *miss*.

What century did he think we were in?

"Party Archive?" I asked.

"Are you after the pre-1990 files or more recent, miss?"

He had me there. I hadn't thought they might be split up like that, but I guess it made sense. I decided to deal with the more recent stuff first, I might find an up-to-date address and it would be interesting to see whether Becker had left the Party before getting involved with the Nazis.

I followed the caretaker's instructions, going up the marble steps and getting lost in the maze of corridors. Upstairs it was a bit less grand, at least in the bits I was wandering around in right now. Just the usual cracked lino, washed-out gloss paint and dust.

I found the right floor at last. A babushka guarded a desk placed across the corridor. She ignored me for a bit—the usual game: see who gives up first. But I wasn't going to play that game today, because I was a State Official.

"I've come to check personnel records."

Without looking up from her magazine the babushka slid a brown piece of paper over to me. I had a quick read through the form, it all looked pretty straightforward.

"Pen?"

"Supply your own," she said, still not bothering to look up from her magazine.

"Could you lend me a pen please?" Nice as pie, I couldn't do it any nicer than that. But there was no answer.

I went back down to the lobby, wishing I had a ball of string with me so that I could find my way back, but in the end it was OK because I found some back stairs that went straight down to the corridor behind the main entrance.

Mr Brown Dust Coat was still there, and seemed happy to lend me his pencil, so I filled in the form while he talked at me about the heatwave. When I'd filled in the easy bits I headed back upstairs, taking the pencil with me. It was only a chewed stump, he probably wouldn't miss it.

The babushka took the form from me, and still flicking through her stupid romance magazine, she laid it on her desk, picked up the stamp and was about to plonk it in the little round circle printed there for the purpose when she finally decided to check what I'd written.

"*Name of person requesting access*: not filled in," she read out aloud. "*File Reference: not known. Dept./Type of File: Cadre Records. Name of Person: Becker.*" She was merciless, reading out every single bit of the form, even those bits I didn't fill in because I didn't know how to or because the questions were stupid.

It was only when she'd finished that she looked at me for the first time. She got a bit of a shock, I don't think she was expecting a punk to be standing in front of her precious desk.

"Is this some kind of joke?" She asked, obviously torn between wanting to carry on with her magazine, and wondering what the hell I was doing there.

"On the contrary, citizen. Here is my authorisation, please bring me the file I requested." I showed her my RS pass, but she didn't seem interested.

"I'm phoning security." She had already picked up the heavy receiver of an old black phone.

I put a finger on the cradle to cut off the call.

"Citizen, I have already told you what I require, and I have shown you my authorisation. Will you do your job or do I have to do it for you?"

"Miss, if you know what's good for you then you'll leave right now. Your authorisation won't get you very far in this building, you've no right to access post-1990 files, those are for internal use only."

Fuck, she could be right—I hadn't thought of that, the Party archives would no longer be a state matter. I might just have overstepped the mark, just a weeny bit.

I grabbed the search form from her hand and got out of there before she could make that telephone call.

Martin

I was in the kitchen when the doorbell rang. Jürgen Kerth
carried on singing as I opened the door to Steinlein.

"Have you thought about it?"

"Give me a chance—we only talked a couple of hours ago."
I went back into the kitchen, leaving the door open for
Steinlein to come in if he chose to. I could hear his cane
tapping across the floor, drowning out Kerth's *He junge
Mutti*. "Actually, I've been enjoying not thinking about it." I
went through to the living room and took the needle off the
record. I hated doing that, but I didn't want Steinlein spoiling
the reggae-meets-blues of one of Kerth's best tracks.

When I got back to the kitchen Steinlein was leaning
against a cabinet. Sweat glistened on his forehead and his
eyes were receding into his skull. I reached past him, took a
glass from the shelf and returned to the sink to fill it with
water.

"Normally I wouldn't be wasting my time on this," he said.
"But as I said before, this source has never been wrong-"

"*If* it's the same source."

"We should assume it is." Steinlein's fingers were tapping
on the kitchen unit, making it hard for me to concentrate on
what he was saying. "This is too big to get wrong. Think
about the timing—the country's like a tinderbox. The
referendum on the Wall last April divided the country, the
Volkskammer is dragging its feet on the constitutional
amendments and then there are the elections coming up in
the autumn. There's no way of telling whether the pro-
unification parties will have a majority, or whether the
Communists will gain power again."

I didn't answer Steinlein, he still had a long way to go if
he wanted to convince me.

"Will you help me out, just for a few days? If we don't
manage to substantiate the threats in that time then I'll leave

you in peace. Deal?"

He looked so tired and desperate that I gave him the glass of water. That and my word that he'd have my help for a few days.

I went back into the living room and the police officer followed me.

"There's been another contact from the source." Steinlein told me as he eased himself down to a hard chair. "It confirms my initial assessment that they're based in the Operational Area. Maybe that's why they're shy. They say they want to be handled by you only, and first contact is to be a brush past."

Handled by me? A brush past? In West Berlin? It was all too far-fetched for my taste. I shook my head, this wasn't what I had in mind when I agreed to help out.

"There was a message waiting for me when I got back to the police station so I came here immediately. The source has specifically asked for you."

"Why me?" I asked, trying to stall him. "Why do they want me?"

"People know you by reputation. They've seen you on the television, in the newspapers. They know what you did during the Silesian affair, and what happened to you in March. People trust you." Steinlein pulled back his sleeve and turned his wrist to check his watch. "The problem is, they want the brush past to happen this afternoon. In fact, if you leave now you might just be in time."

I crossed over to the westbound platform at Friedrichstrasse station and boarded the S-Bahn just as the signal sounded and the doors ground shut. As always, I looked down at the Wall as we passed over it, then the still waters of the Humboldt Harbour, bright under the high sun. Recently I'd been to West Berlin a lot, visiting my daughter or on some liaison matter, but the other half of the city still didn't feel like home, not the way East Berlin did.

The train slowed as it entered Lehrter Stadt station and stood for a while as we changed drivers. Watching the drivers exchange a handshake and a few words I thought about what it meant to cross the Wall. In East Berlin I knew the people, the streets, I knew the rules. But West Berlin was a foreign country. Same language, similar streets, but a different system. It made me nervous at the best of times, but now I was in the West on an operation my previous anxieties were being put into perspective.

I swallowed my fear and a couple of stops later I got off.

Down at street level I walked along the wide boulevard, heading for the flea market. *Right-hand middle aisle*, I whispered to myself, *Brass goods*. I made my way through the stalls, many selling memorabilia from my own country: military and MfS uniforms, Party books, medals. Other stalls sold items that were still used in many households over in the East, but had here gained an attractive patina of antiquity: meat grinders, mangles, desk pencil sharpeners, fruit juice pans. I pushed through the sweating crowds, keeping an eye open for the brass goods stall. Once there I stood still, pretending to admire the horse brasses, milk jugs and jewellery boxes while the mass of punters edged around me on their hunt for bargains and souvenirs.

I was wondering how long I'd have to stand there, looking at overpriced tat that I neither wanted nor could afford, when I was shunted into the other people looking at the stall. I staggered, and some *Wessi* pushed me back, muttering about clumsy *Ossis*. I regained my balance and my hand went to my trouser pocket, checking my wallet was still there. It was, but my hand also found a piece of folded paper. I pulled it out, not looking at it, just feeling it between thumb and fingers—it was just a scrap, folded over a few times. I pushed it deeper into my pocket and made my way out of the melee.

At the edge of the flea market I paused, glancing back. No way of knowing who had given me the note. Was it the oaf who had barged into me, or had somebody already slipped it into my pocket before that? I pulled the note out, not opening it up, just looking at it. Grey, recycled paper, lined like schoolkids use, and now blotted with damp marks from my sweaty fingers.

I had my prize, first mission successfully completed. I could return home.

At Bellevue station half a dozen West Berlin police officers boarded. They passed slowly down the train asking to see identity papers. They didn't ask everyone, just those of us from the East. I showed them my PM 12, which caused some frowning and nose wrinkling.

"Why do you only have temporary documents?"

"My *Ausweis* was stolen a few weeks ago, I haven't been issued with a new one yet."

The policeman went to confer with a colleague, one with more stars on his epaulettes. He took my PM 12 with him. They stood discussing the issue for a few moments, long enough for the train to pull into Lehrter Stadt station, last stop before the Wall. The police officers got off the train, all except the one with my papers. He was still flicking through the few pages, pretending to look for something. His colleagues were standing on the platform, smoking and watching us through the carriage windows. Up and down the carriage the passengers were pretending not to stare. I ignored the contempt in the eyes of Westerners irritated by the hold-up, I blocked out the sympathy and fear of those from the East, old memories too close to the surface.

"Are you a police officer?" he demanded. "Or a member of the security organs of the GDR?"

I shook my head, mentally double checking that I'd thought to leave my RS pass at home.

Another flick through my PM 12, a stare at the photograph, comparing it to my face, the young policeman trying to make the decision: take me off the train for questioning, or let me go. A glance out of the window at his impatient colleagues and without another word he thrust my papers at me and left the train.

The red signal next to the door lit up, the two-tone bell rang. The doors grated shut between me and the West Berlin cops. I started breathing again as the train accelerated, whining out of the station, over the harbour basin, over the Wall, back home to the East.

15:55
Martin

Once I'd changed trains at Friedrichstrasse I unfolded the note. Small, neat capitals were written in blue ballpoint pen:

VME/E/1059/89

That was it, just a series of numbers and letters. Looked like a file reference, and I knew where I could find plenty of files that had been catalogued that way. If I was quick I could get there before they shut.

Half an hour later I was in the reading room of the Normannenstrasse complex where the Stasi used to have their headquarters. The archivist had gone off to the stacks holding the search form on which I'd entered the reference from the note along with a few made-up numbers.

After ten minutes the archivist returned, shaking her head. "I'll need more time for some of these files, about half are missing, some aren't even referenced. I'll check them against the central indexes, but here's the ones I've got so far."

She piled a good forty or fifty centimetres of files onto my reading desk then wheeled her trolley away.

I was the only person in the reading room, no-one there to observe what I was doing, so I went straight to the file I was here for. The first four or five pages were details of sources, action plans, all the usual Stasi procedures. The seventh page was a letter, addressed to General Mielke, the head of the Stasi. It was typed on German State Theatre letter-paper, and informed Mielke of an artists' resolution condemning the violent behaviour of the security organs during the fortieth anniversary of the Republic in October 1989.

I turned to the last sheet. It was the final page of the minutes for the meeting where the artists' resolution had been agreed. This was just history—was I on a wild goose chase? Fighting off resignation, I flicked through the file again, looking for pages that seemed out of place. And there they were, same kind of paper, but the text from a different typewriter. I scanned these pages: minutes of various meetings, no names of participants, no circulation list, just summaries of what had been said. The language was different, more formal, and the subject of the discussions was identified only as *Zielperson*, target. There were no clear indications about who that target might be, just enough hints to keep me interested.

I extracted these extra pages, folding them into my jacket pocket before putting the file in the middle of the pile on the desk. I opened another folder at random and left it there. Time to get back to Stralau and have a good look at what I'd found, but first I wanted to know who had last accessed that file. I left the reading room and went to the archivist's office. No-one answered my knock so I let myself in, quietly shutting the door behind me. The room was tiny, barely enough space for the desk, chair and filing cabinet that filled it. My search request lay in a tray on the desk. On the shelves below I found the forms for previous days, neatly filed away in ring-binders. Ticking through the pages, I scanned file references, looking for my file. I'd checked the last seven days and was about to open another binder when I heard a door click shut, somewhere further down the corridor. My ears tensed to the approaching noises: feet slapping along the linoleum, the sounds growing sharper and louder. The door shivered as the handle was depressed. There was nowhere to hide in the small office, no cupboards, no corners. My eyes fell to the floor, still searching for possibilities as the door began to open.

I slipped behind the door, wondering whether I was doing the right thing, whether I should just pull my RS pass and start making demands. The door stopped, and I heard voices, first a low mumble, and then the higher pitch of the archivist: "Wait in the reading room, I'll bring them over."

The door opened further and an arm reached in, depositing a search form in the tray on the desk. The arm withdrew again, the door pulled closed behind it. The slapping footsteps faded as the archivist went back to the stacks.

Before leaving, I had a look at the new search form. The name meant nothing to me: DVP Sergeant Heubach. I copied my own search onto a new form, omitting the reference to the file I'd just looked at, and swapped it for the original. I headed out, making sure not to bump into the archivist or Sergeant Heubach.

17:28
Martin

Once back at the Stralau office I had a good look at the papers I'd found: extracts from at least three different sets of minutes and a situation report. The cover pages from each file were missing, so I had to guess at their chronological order, but I reckoned the first in the sequence was to do with a discussion about whether Kaminsky should be nominated to the Executive Committee of the Party. He was never mentioned by name, but the context was enough for me to be fairly sure they were talking about him. The meeting had concerns that Kaminsky was a loose cannon: his politics were unclear, but he was a good speaker, and he was gaining support among the Party's grassroots. According to the dense prose I was scanning, the main reason Kaminsky was allowed to join the Executive Committee was that he was deemed too dangerous to leave on the outside. The hope was that by giving him more responsibility he would somehow become more manageable.

I turned to the next set of minutes. Once again the meeting was of a small group of senior Party members. Within weeks of Kaminsky joining the Party's executive this group was regretting the decision. There was talk of encouraging him to step down, and if he wouldn't take a hint then the group would make use of compromising material to force his hand.

I looked at the situation report next. It was written by some kind of Party intelligence or analytics department, and documented the rising popularity of Kaminsky. His appeal among various demographics was tabulated by Party membership (pre- and post-1989), employment categories and geographic area. Kaminsky seemed to enjoy strong support among those who'd left the Party in 1989 and 1990, mainly in the south and east of Saxony, and to a lesser extent in Saxony-Anhalt and eastern Thuringia.

The final set of minutes were the most interesting. It was a short document, less than one side. Kaminsky was threatening to set up his own political movement, and to take the Party's members with him. The *Bonzen* in the Party weren't prepared to allow that to happen and it sounded like they were ready to play hard ball: *The committee needs to consider what measures are at their disposal in order to achieve long-term disciplinary effects on the subject.*

Karo

"You again?"

"Yeah, well, I was just passing."

"Passing West Berlin?" Katrin laughed and held the door open.

"I really messed up today, I think I might be in trouble," I told her.

Katrin was great, she listened to me blether on about my major fuck-up in the Party archives, and then she pointed out that since RS is being wound up anyway there's nothing really bad that can happen.

I wish I could be more like her, she was just so calm and she brought me back down and spotted the important bits straight off, showed me I'd been tying myself up in knots over nothing.

"Something else is bothering you, isn't it?" she asked after we'd sorted out the non-problem of my visit to the archives.

I didn't answer, but went into the kitchen to get some water. Katrin leaned against the door as I let the tap run cold and filled a glass.

"Is it about your friend?"

I took a sip and nodded, still not looking at Katrin. She came over and put her arms around me.

"He told me some really awful stuff last night. He talked about it a bit and then left me bawling away in a graveyard," I mumbled into her shoulder.

Katrin took the glass off me and manoeuvred me into the living room. With soft hands she pressed me onto the couch.

"Want to talk about it?"

I shook my head. What Schimmel had told me was personal, I wouldn't go blabbing about it.

But then Katrin took a different tack: "Do you identify with him, with whatever it is that happened to him?"

Her question confused me, I'd never experienced anything

half as bad as what Schimmel told me about last night. I shook my head.

"But you're quite similar to him, aren't you?" She saw my face and rephrased the question. "You said Schimmel left home when he was still a kid, and from what you've said in the past I kind of got the impression that the same thing happened to you."

"It's not the same!" I jumped up and faced Katrin. "Schimmel grew up in the middle of nowhere and ran away from home at thirteen. He spent years in a borstal because of that!"

"It's OK if you don't want to talk about it, I was just wondering ..." Katrin had her hands out, inviting me back onto the couch.

"I was sixteen when I left home so there was nothing they could do about it." I sat down again, but leant forward, elbows on my knees. I couldn't see Katrin, but could feel her right next to me. "Anyway, it was my dad. He chucked me out. Only good thing he ever did. Said I was a disgrace."

"You weren't happy at home?"

A bitter laugh. "Happy? How could I be, with that bastard sniping at me all the time. Nothing was ever good enough for him. I remember one time I brought home a report card from school, I'd got a 1 or 2 in every subject except Russian. I'd only managed a 3, but I was dead proud of it, because I really struggled in Russian. Know what he said? Know what the bastard said? *Won't get very far with these grades.* You can imagine how I felt." I held my hand out, the tip of my index finger and thumb almost touching. "That small."

Katrin leaned forward, trying to see my face. I ignored her.

"Nothing was ever good enough for him. Whatever I did, no matter how hard I tried, it didn't mean shit, just another reason to make snide remarks. So after a lifetime of trying to please him I just gave up. I didn't bother trying any more. I said *Fuck you* to him and his bullying, and I said *Fuck you* to the rest of the world, too."

"Is that when you left home?"

"I went with a friend to a punk concert at the *KvU*. Everyone there was screaming *Fuck you*, loud as they could. For the first time ever it felt like I belonged. I didn't need anyone to love me or care about what I did. I didn't need anyone to tell me I'd done well, because I was shouting *Fuck you* as loud as I could."

This time I let Katrin put her arms round me and we both flopped back against the cushions. It felt good to be held. It felt safe. But even though it felt good I couldn't help but be envious of Katrin, having Martin as a dad.

"Maybe that's why I like Martin, maybe he's the dad I never had, he accepts me," I told her.

"He likes you, he thinks you're great."

"But I push him away all the time. I'm mean to him. Sarcastic. I don't want to be but it's like my own dad is in here," I banged my chest with a closed fist. "He's inside me, making me push away the people I like. I'm not very good at people being nice to me, and you and Martin have never been anything but totally nice to me. Ever since I met Martin he's respected me, no matter how stupid or resentful I've been."

Katrin turned my face towards her, palms against my chin, fingers up my cheeks. Her skin smelt of roses. "I like you. And you won't ever push me away, no matter how hard you try."

We stayed like that for a moment, looking into each other's eyes, but then I got embarrassed and eased myself out of her clasp. I stood up and fished a cassette out of my rucksack.

"Here, I made you a mix-tape."

Katrin took it off me, turning it round to look at the picture I'd drawn for the insert. "Punk?"

"No. Well yes, a bit. But not really—you're gonna like it,

there's nothing heavy, no Schleimkeim or anything like that, but there's some Fall, and a bit of PJ and the first track is ace, it's by Stereolab, and I taped some KLF and Feeling B and ..." I was babbling. I tailed off, coming over all embarrassed again, but Katrin pretended not to notice.

She hugged the cassette to her chest. "I've got one for you too." She reached behind her and picked up a tape. "Everything But The Girl—their new album. It's what we were listening to yesterday."

I took the tape off her and made a move for the hi-fi, but Katrin shot across the room, trying to get there before me.

"Mix-tape first!"

I grabbed her by the shoulder, turning her onto her back and climbing over her, reaching out for the tape deck. She put her arms around me, dragging me down and giggling as I collapsed onto her. We were rolling round the floor like a couple of toddlers, laughing the whole time.

"Ssshh, the neighbours!" There was a knocking, it sounded like someone had taken off their shoe and was banging it on the wall, telling us to shut the fuck up, but that just made us laugh even harder. With a sudden wriggle Katrin slid out from under me, reaching out and slotting my mix tape into the machine.

"Sneaky!" We were both still sprawled across the floor, our faces almost touching. I was hyper-aware of her warm breath tickling my nose, of her eyes looking into mine. I didn't think about it, I just moved my head closer. She didn't move away from me, she waited, mouth slightly open, expectant.

My hand sought hers, but it found her thigh first, and with another giggle Katrin wormed away, landing on the couch. She pulled her feet up, hugging her knees while she squirmed her bottom into the corner, leaning against the armrest.

The guitars of Stereolab's *French Disko* had kicked in now, with the vocals gliding up behind, and I moved over to sit next to Katrin. There was silence for a bit while we pretended to listen to the lyrics from opposite ends of the couch.

I could feel Katrin's eyes on me, but I looked off into a corner where some tie-dyed material was hanging on the wall.

"I'm not like that. You do know that, don't you?" Katrin had unfolded her legs a little, she was still at one end of the couch, but her feet were on the cushions next to my thighs. It was like heat was beaming out of her toes, I could feel it through my jeans.

"Is anyone?" I laughed and put my fingers over Katrin's toes. They wiggled a bit, but didn't move away, so I started massaging them, rubbing each in turn.

"But are *you*?" Katrin still had her gaze fixed on me, I was watching my hands knead her feet.

"Who needs labels?"

Katrin's toes wiggled again.

18:44
Martin

Steinlein's tall frame filled the doorway, his stick slanted away from his body, pointing the way towards his desk.

He stood for a few moments, looking not towards me or the papers I'd found in the Stasi archives, but out of the window, at the park on the other side of the river.

I placed the minutes on Steinlein's desk and thought about what I'd read. We would have to check the material's provenance—if the papers were authentic then they'd corroborate Steinlein's theory that the Party was plotting to get rid of Kaminsky. That seemed barely believable, but verifying the intelligence would be a first step towards preventing an assassination. My thoughts were interrupted by Steinlein clearing his throat.

"Any trouble over there?" he asked as he stepped towards

his desk.

"West German cops were doing ID checks. They didn't like my temporary *Ausweis*."

"And?"

"No problems. But there's no way I'm going over there again."

Steinlein didn't seem concerned, he was too busy following his own thoughts. "Did you see the source? Did you recognise him?"

I shook my head.

"Shame," said Steinlein, but he'd already started reading.

"Those minutes seem to support your theory."

Instead of answering, Steinlein just gave a grunt. He was holding a sheet of paper up to the light. "Did you see this?" He put the paper back on the desk, his finger poised over an area of text.

I moved in to see what he was pointing at, and as I did so his finger moved closer to the paper. He was indicating nothing but the gap between two lines. I couldn't see anything unusual, the lines were regularly spaced, except the alignment of the letter e was slightly out of sync with other characters, edging up into the white space that so interested Steinlein.

"Hold it to the light," he said.

I took the sheet and held it up. And there, just where Steinlein had indicated, were faint pencil markings.

Tacheles 0905. 2nd window main staircase. Poster.

"Looks like you'll be collecting some post in the morning."

"Why are you doing this?" I asked him.

He looked up, not understanding.

"Why are you handling the case in this way? Unofficially, from here?"

"I've told you, I'm concerned about potential police involvement in the plot against Kaminsky."

"But it could still be handled internally. You could talk to your superior. Who do you report to anyway, is it Captain Neumann?"

"I don't know who's involved, it could be anyone-"

"What's in it for you? Do you actually care what happens to Kaminsky or is this just about preventing a crime?"

Steinlein didn't respond for a moment or two, considering how to answer. "What he says makes a lot of sense."

He had stopped reading, he was waiting for my reaction.

"You support him?" I hadn't even considered that Steinlein might find Kaminsky and his policies acceptable.

"I'm a policeman, not a politician—my job is to protect the people of the GDR. I don't get involved in politics."

How could any even half-way intelligent person support Kaminsky? Wasn't it obvious that he was just on a power trip, that he didn't really have the best interests of the country at heart?

"You have to admit this country's an absolute mess. Kaminsky's right when he says we need strong leadership, we're never going to get anywhere with the Round Tables interfering all the time. Any influence from outside the government and the *Volkskammer* is undemocratic."

"Do you seriously believe that Kaminsky will be good for the GDR?" I asked him.

"He has the support of the people, who am I to question that?"

Kaminsky wanted to roll back everything we had achieved since 1989, and Steinlein was basically telling me he agreed with that. I was shocked by the realisation that the policeman and I wanted such different things for our country.

I physically took a step back from him, then turned and left the building.

Day 4
Wednesday
15th June 1994

I'm doing something different, and I have your support to do that. Yet there are also doubters, nay-sayers who don't like what's happening: the reactionaries, saboteurs, anti-social elements and anti-democrats—the ones who can't accept the will of the people.
They may not accept the situation, but I accept them.
I tolerate them and their outdated attitudes because I know that the people of the GDR will overcome this irresponsible resistance.
But I can't accept state agencies interfering in democratic processes. I've been informed that there has been an attempt to access my cadre files in the Party archive. Not an attempt by one of those meddling journalists—no, it is far more serious than that.
This attempt to gain illegal access to the Party archive was by a member of a government agency.
Not just any government agency, but the Republikschutz itself.
Agencies like the RS are undermining our country. The RS may claim to uphold democracy but they are unaccountable, secretive and dangerous.
That is why the people voted to wind up the RS. Yet here we are, more than ten weeks after the referendum, and the RS are still going about their dubious business.
This is not acceptable. Let me be clear: the RS is not democratic. It is a danger to our democracy and we cannot allow it to continue to defy the will of the people.

Martin

Steinlein had said it himself: if Kaminsky were assassinated this country would rip itself apart. Steinlein and I wanted not just different things for our country, what we wanted was incompatible. Yet despite our opposing political views, neither of us wanted the GDR to descend into chaos.

That's why, just after half-past eight this morning, I caught the S-Bahn to Friedrichstrasse. Despite the early hour the roads and pavements around the station were hot, the tram tracks shimmered into the distance.

I'd deal with Steinlein later, I decided. First we had to prevent Kaminsky from being assassinated. Once we'd done that I'd take them both down.

My destination wasn't far: a half-ruin just at the beginning of Oranienburger Strasse. Tacheles, they called it. I'd never been there but I'd heard about it, even seen it on a culture programme on Western TV. A group of artists had squatted the building in 1990, just before it was due to be demolished. They did emergency repairs and moved in, using the building as ateliers and exhibition space, as well as the inevitable political meetings.

The main entrance was shrouded in wooden scaffolding, a wide staircase led off the foyer. As the note said, there was a poster taped to the window on the second half-landing. There was nobody about, still too early for the artists.

I clasped my cigarette between my lips, squinting through the smoke as I eased the tape off the bottom left-hand corner of the poster. I pushed my fingers underneath the paper and felt around until I snagged a small square of paper. I slid it out. Another look up and down the stairs, then I was off, back onto the street.

I walked a few blocks before ducking into a cellar doorway, wondering whether I should have suggested to Steinlein that he come along too, hang back and try to spot the source. But I knew what his response would have been: *It's about trust*, he would say. But that was my problem, I didn't see any reason to trust our so-called source, and I had serious doubts about my partner too.

I unfolded the note, same paper, same neat printed letters as last time: *Prinzenstrasse open-air swimming pool 12:30. Bring 400 DM*

Prinzenstrasse was the same road as Heinrich-Heine-Strasse, the name changed when you crossed into West Berlin. I was fairly sure the open-air baths were right at the far end, by the Landwehr canal, but I could do with checking a map, not to mention finding 400 Westmarks. I phoned Steinlein from a phone box.

"I told you not to contact me!"

"It's OK, I gave the switchboard a false name. Listen, the source wants 400 DM. He wants to meet in Kreuzberg just after midday." I listened to the static on the line, waiting for Steinlein's answer.

"Meet me. Warschauer Platz, eleven-thirty." Steinlein's words were chased down the line by the click of his phone being hung up.

When I got back to my flat there was a message on the notebook that hung on the door. *Not seen you in ages* (underlined twice) *let's have beer and a catch up!* There was no signature, but I recognised the scrawl as Karo's.

I tore the message off the pad and went inside. Beer and a catch-up, even though she'd only been here the other day? She probably wanted to talk about whatever was happening at RS. But right now I didn't have time, I had work to do.

The phone rang while I was in the kitchen pulling a towel off the clothes horse. I ignored it, going instead into my bed-room to find swimming trunks. I was in too much of a rush and in no mood to talk to whoever was on the other end.

The phone was still ringing as I left the flat.

Karo

That was probably the worst experience of my life. I mean, morning meetings are *always* awful, but this one ... After what had happened yesterday I knew Laura would have a go at me but it was Klaus who was really laying it on thick.

"I didn't know! How was I supposed to know? It's not like I asked for Kaminsky's files!"

"No, but he's been on the news claiming you were. We're doing you a favour here, letting you work on your own case —and this is how you repay us? A little bit of discretion is all that we asked for, but what do-"

"Nobody said nothing about discretion!"

There was a gap in all the ranting and shouting, which is where Erika stepped in. "Clearly Karo didn't realise she was overstepping the mark. Perhaps we should look to ourselves, ask whether we failed in our responsibilities—such as making sure that Karo knows what she can and can't do?"

I was well relieved when Erika said that, she was letting me off the hook. But then she turned to me and I held my breath, nervous about what she'd say next.

"And as for you, Karo, I take it you've realised the need for discretion?" She waited until I gave a reluctant nod. "And that if you're not one hundred percent sure about anything— anything at all—that you come and talk to one of us?" A hard look was on her face.

"OK."

"So shall we regard this episode as closed?" Erika asked the meeting.

"How can we?" Klaus still wasn't happy. "There's all sorts of fallout we can expect from this mess."

I wanted to stomp out, leave them to their stupid messes, but I didn't want to piss them off any more than I already had done. I needed to keep my RS pass for a bit longer. So I sat there while they droned on about potentially sensitive scenarios and stuff—on and on, worrying about things that probably would never even happen. It all sounded like a load of paranoid bollocks to me. But then again, they had a good idea of what to expect from our fucked up political system.

As soon as I got out of the meeting I gave Martin a ring, I needed to let off steam about his colleagues. I let the phone ring for ages and ages but he didn't answer, even though he must have been at home. I mean where else would he be if not at home? I slammed the receiver down.

"Typical Martin, not there when I need him. I'm always there for him, but the first time I actually need him-" I was talking out loud, like some batty old dame, but broke off when I saw Erika standing in the doorway to my—Martin's—office.

"Who are you grumbling about now?"

"You. Who else?" I answered. But I was still thinking of Martin and what I'd told Katrin yesterday, about pushing people away. I wanted to do things differently from now on, which is why I'd already been to his flat this morning, y'know, just to say hi. But he'd been out. Or asleep. I left a message, I thought he would have phoned me back by now.

Erika came right into the office. "I just wanted to check in with you, ask if there's anything I can do to help?"

"What with?"

"Becker. It was his files you wanted to see at the archive, wasn't it?"

I nodded glumly. It felt like the whole world knew I'd failed on that score.

"If you'd talked to us first we would have told you about the difficulties with accessing the Party archives." I crossed my arms, mentally preparing myself for another lecture, but Erika had other ideas. "So now you need to be a bit more subtle and you'll have to cover your tracks better. Look, this Becker—you say he was director of the juvenile temporary secure home? Well there will be files at the Ministry for People's Education, so you can start there. If I were you I'd start by asking general questions about similar institutions, get them to bring a whole load of files to look through. Take your time, circle in, look at all the staff, starting from before Becker was working there-"

"And make it look like I'm not actually interested in Becker in particular? Erika, you're a genius!"

11:25
Karo

Before leaving for the Ministry for People's Education I gave Martin another ring, but still no answer. I didn't waste too much time on wondering where he might be—I had my own mission right now, and I was prepared: I had a plan and I had a pen.

I showed my RS pass at the main desk of the ministry, went down to the archive in the basement and asked for a Search Request Form. Feeling proud of myself for being so oblique I asked for staff lists for all the Special Homes, *Durchgangsheime* and Borstals in the districts of Berlin, Frankfurt and Potsdam. Under Reason For Search I put *restitution claims*. That sounded dry enough, I reckoned.

I had to wait for about ten minutes before the archivist creaked in, pushing a squealing trolley. She had about a thousand files, all boxed up in heavy, grey cartons. So much for being oblique, it was going to take me all day to find what I needed! I waited for the creaky lady to disappear again before getting a bottle of beer out of my rucksack. I hadn't even got the top off when I heard a clucking from behind me.

"Just what do you think you are doing, young lady? This is an archive, not a bar. Either you put that away or you leave!" She carried on rattling away about what the world's coming to and who'd have thought. I put the bloody bottle away, and opened the first box, and after a vicious stare the archivist crept away again. She'd probably gone to spy on me from her cubbyhole.

It took me a while to find the file for the *Durchgangsheim* here in Berlin, but the good news was that the archivist had been too lazy to sort out just the files I'd requested and had actually brought every single staff-related file, including the cadre files. So I found Becker and all his details in no time at all: Andreas Becker, deputy-director from October 1987 until the end of 1988, just over a year. On paper, he had impressive qualifications: study in Köthen, then awarded a doctorate by the College of Education in Potsdam. Later on he became a member of the Academy of Pedagogical Sciences and the Institution for Pedagogical Psychology.

A big fish, in other words.

I unclipped his photograph and slipped it into my pocket then made some notes about his qualifications and stuff. There was loads of boring stuff in there, like how he volunteered to help the police and the FDJ when he was a student, stuff like that, and I nearly didn't bother copying that down. In the end I decided to. There was no up-to-date address or telephone number, but it was still a good start.

I flicked through the other files for a bit, but I had what I needed. I stacked the archive boxes back on the trolley and left.

11:29
Martin

Most of Warschauer Platz is behind the boundary wall of the Narva lightbulb works. The little that remains open to the public lies between canyons of factory buildings and the derelict U-Bahn station. From down here I could see neither the capped brickwork of the nearby Oberbaum bridge nor Berlin's first high-rise building, the Narva Tower, just a few metres away. In fact, from down here I could see only sooty walls and the solitary figure of Steinlein halfway down the Platz. Instead of a greeting he pressed an envelope into my hand.

"Here's the money. Whatever information the source gives you, bring it straight back. Hide it well, be careful it's not found at the border."

"Hello to you, too."

"This is not the time for jokes, Martin." Steinlein was looking around the whole time, keeping an eye on any passers-by. "I don't know what you're playing at, but walking out while we're in the middle of a conversation isn't something I take kindly to."

"Look, I'm sorry about last night-"

"When you get to your rendezvous wait for the source to come to you. Relax, don't pay too much attention to your surroundings. Let the source play it the way he wants to. If you get a chance to speak to him then tell him we need more information, that we can pay. We need anything he has on Kaminsky, anything at all. Got that?"

"He?"

"What?"

"You said *he*. Is the informant male?"

"Figure of speech, we don't know. Now get going. I'll be at the Stralau office from three o'clock, I'll wait for you there."

Under normal circumstances I would have been at the Prinzenstrasse baths in plenty of time, but as soon as I reached the border crossing at Oberbaum bridge I could tell that these weren't normal circumstances.

"You'll have a bit of a wait at the other end," the young border policeman told me as I passed his post at the Eastern end of the bridge.

"What's going on?" A queue snaked back towards us, there seemed to be some hold up at the gate in the Wall at the far end.

"West Berlin police are checking everybody's documents, they've taken some people away for questioning."

"Why? Who are they questioning?"

The guard shrugged, he didn't know and he didn't really care.

I remembered the police officers on the S-Bahn yesterday, the way one of them had been suspicious of my temporary *Ausweis*. Perhaps this wasn't the best day to head into West Berlin, but I didn't have any choice if I wanted to meet the source.

I joined the end of the queue, just a dozen or so people in front of me, so hopefully this wouldn't take too long.

But ten minutes later we were still no further. We stood under the midday sun, and I looked over the parapet at the river below, thinking about the swimming trunks in my shoulder bag. The grey water flowed past, ochre foam collecting by the banks.

"Did you come for the view or are you in the queue?" A Berlin voice behind me demanded.

I looked up, the line in front of me was moving again. Now there was just a couple of people between me and the Wall. We shuffled forwards, and finally I was through the gate and over the white line that marked the border. But we weren't finished with queueing, we were hemmed in by crowd control fences which led us round to the left where a couple of policemen stood. Behind them was a hut, I'd never noticed it before, but the grey paint that peeled from its wooden sides told me it had always been there.

The West Berlin police officers were carefully checking everyone's papers, just as they had done on the train. I held out my temporary *Ausweis*, it was taken off me and each page was carefully examined.

"Holger?" The policeman held my *Ausweis* up for his colleague to check, but Holger nodded.

"Bitte sehr. Der nächste!"

And that was it. I was through.

I hurried along the road towards the U-Bahn station, climbing the steps to the platform and jumping on the train just as the bell rang.

I looked at my watch, I was already late for my meeting.

12:57

Martin

I got off the U-Bahn at Prinzenstrasse and jogged through the traffic to the entrance of the swimming pool. Join the end of another queue, hand over my precious Westmarks, through the turnstile and I was in the open-air baths. I stood just inside, not sure where to go or what to do next. For the last few hours I'd been focussing on getting here on time. But here I was, half an hour late. No welcoming committee, nobody waiting, no-one holding a sign with my name on it.

Not knowing what else to do, I did the obvious. I changed into my trunks, left my clothes and bag in a locker and followed the path to the pools.

A group of Turkish lads were kicking a football around a grassy area dotted with trees, but most people were either in the water or sunbathing. I found a bit of shade and sat down, looking at the hundreds of people, wondering whether the source was among them, watching me. I put my straw hat on the grass and discreetly slipped the envelope of money under it.

I had my watch with me, and I checked my wrist often, marking each minute as it idled by. Part of me couldn't see the point in hanging around any longer, I'd arrived late and the source had probably long gone by the time I'd sat down on the grass. The only thing I was going to get here was heatstroke.

Ten minutes passed, then fifteen. How long should I wait?

★

Sometime after two o'clock I gave up. I'd been there for more than enough time for contact to be made, it clearly wasn't going to happen. I took another look around, trying to spot anyone by themselves, anyone looking shifty in any way, but could see only couples and families. Apart from me, nobody was by themselves.

It wasn't until I stood up that I noticed the plastic carrier bag next to my hat. It hadn't been there when I sat down, and it certainly wasn't mine—a bright red bag from the Kaisers supermarket chain. I looked around, but there was no-one nearby, no-one to whom it could belong. I picked up my hat, the envelope underneath was missing. My contact hadn't missed me, he'd just been discreet.

"Come with us."

The two men were waiting outside the changing rooms when I came out. They were police, that much was clear from their manner and their clothes—they weren't wearing uniforms, but they might as well have been. The only thing wrong was that they had spoken English, not German. I couldn't be totally sure I'd understood exactly what they'd said, but their purpose was clear.

"Who are you?" I managed in English.

"Come with us, all will be explained." The voice was polite, but the way the two men stepped closer to me left me in no doubt what I was expected to do.

13:21
Karo

After the dusty boredom of the archive I decided to drop in on Katrin on the way home. No biggie if she wasn't there, I just thought it would be nice to say hi.

I got some hassle off the West Berlin cop standing at the border crossing. It wasn't anything major, nothing I've not dealt with a million times before, but since when did they hassle us going *into* West Berlin? Anyway, it was all good in the end, because I bumped into Katrin in her tenement entryway just as I was coming back down the stairs. I'd already been up to her flat but there had been no answer, because here she was, walking in off the street.

"Karo, oh!"

"I was just passing ..."

"Yeah, sure. Nice surprise."

"It's fine if you're busy, y'know if you've got stuff to do ..."

Katrin took hold of my hand, the gesture timid—it was well cute, and we went up the stairs to her flat. We went in and I curled up on her sofa, hoping she'd come and snuggle up with me, but she called through the door as she went into the kitchen.

"I'm making a pot of tea—want some?"

I followed her into the kitchen where she was standing by the kettle, staring into space.

I watched her for a minute before asking if she was OK.

Katrin started, as if she hadn't realised I was standing next to her, then turned to me, putting her hands on my hips and drawing me close. I lifted my head so she could kiss me but she was staring into space again, somewhere over my shoulder.

"What's up, Katrin?"

No answer.

"Is it about yesterday, about what we did? Because if-"

Katrin gave me a smile, it was a really nice smile, except it didn't quite reach her eyes. "Just got a lot on my mind, that's all. Everything's fine."

I wasn't sure what to do. I thought Katrin was happy about what had happened between us, I mean, it was lovely. We had fun, it felt good. Maybe it was because I ran off so early? Maybe I should have stayed longer?

"Because if this is about yesterday-"

Katrin stroked my head, the bit on the side where the hair is cut really short. "I like the spikiness," she said. "It tickles my hand."

I switched the kettle off and took her hands in mine, pulling her gently into the living room, towards the sofa. Our eyes locked and her smile came back, a real one this time. That amazing Katrin smile.

14:12
Martin

I've no idea where I was taken. I was in the car for quite a while, half an hour, probably longer, sandwiched in the back between the two men. It gave me some time to consider my position.

They knew my name. They looked like cops, they sounded like cops and wore their clothes like cops. But they weren't cops, not West Berlin cops. They were Brits or Amis, which meant intelligence services. Whatever was happening to me right now was because of the Kaisers bag.

But on the other hand there had been no attempt to take it off me yet, it was still in my satchel.

The men had refused to identify themselves, in fact, there had been no further interaction once they'd persuaded me to go along with them. I'd considered shouting, making a scene, hoping the crowd of West Berliners at the baths would notice, perhaps even try to help. But the men's use of English had thrown me, and frankly, I hadn't fancied my chances.

The car stopped and the two men got out. One held the door open for me.

"Mr. Grobe, this way please."

I followed the two men down a concrete path, between green lawns and low brick buildings. Going by the general shabbiness of the complex I decided my captors were British rather than American. I clutched my bag all the tighter and considered my situation. We were on a British military base, which I found preferable to a West Berlin police station—I was more optimistic that I wouldn't simply disappear here. But there were no guarantees.

"I demand to speak to Major Clarie," I said, hoping my liaison partner in British Defence Intelligence could intervene. But my guards didn't react to my demands, they just continued to herd me along the concrete path.

We entered one of the whitewashed buildings and in my agitation I tripped over the step, dropping my satchel and nearly falling to the floor. One of the guards rescued the bag but neither of them offered me a hand. Round a corner in the corridor then I was shoved into a room. I turned around as the metal door banged shut behind me.

Drab walls and a low ceiling pressed in upon me. Instead of a window there was a narrow sheet of metal up in a corner, a series of holes allowing air into my cell. A plastic mat lay on a concrete bed, and a bucket stood in the corner.

This wasn't so different from the cells the Stasi had kept me in. There was nothing I could do but wait. Wait and think.

17:10
Karo

I didn't want to outstay my welcome and left quite soon. I loved being with Katrin and I was kinda optimistic that the feeling was mutual. But a voice inside me was still telling me not too push too hard, too fast. I was going to give her a bit of space, I wasn't going to rush her. It was all going to be worth it.

You know that warm feeling you get when you think of a particular person and your stomach goes up and down as if it's the lift of the Television Tower? That's how it was for me that night. I was pushing my bike up Warschauer Strasse, literally miles away, thinking about nothing but Katrin, but Kaminsky brought me back down to earth sharpish. It wasn't literally him, just his fuckwit followers. They were marching down Frankfurter Allee, towards Alexanderplatz, holding a demo with their pathetic banners and torches. As well as the usual red flags they had all sorts of vomit-inducing slogans:

Stop the Asylum Flood!
Jobs for Germans!
Expel the Elite!
Real Democracy Now!

I mean, seriously, who believes this crap? How stupid do you have to be to fall for this shite?

But there was something like a thousand people on the march, and all of them eager to swallow Kaminsky's smooth turds of propaganda.

And the worst thing was the chanting: *Kaminsky Kaminsky Kaminsky*, like he was some Messiah, the answer to all our problems!

But then, just when I thought it couldn't get any worse, it did. I instinctively edged back behind the crowd of onlookers: what I was seeing shouldn't have been a shock, but hearing rumours, and reports on the telephone about what's happening somewhere like Weimar—that's not the same as seeing it on the streets of your home town.

A block of skinheads was bringing up the rear of the demo. Skinny stonewash jeans, green bomber jackets, shaven heads, the full works. Except they were wearing black, red and yellow armbands, and most of them were carrying the old GDR flag—the one that wasn't used any more, the one with the hammer and compass in the middle. They were waving them around and smirking at passers-by. Swaggering about, right arms jabbing the air, thinking they owned Berlin.

Made me want to vomit.

Karo

I was sitting on the floor, listening to a tape of Paranoia, the hardest music I had. Seeing the skins and Kaminsky's marchers together had really put a downer on my day, made me see everything in a negative way. Not only was I pissed off about the idiots and the fash, but I'd started obsessing about Katrin: had she been a bit off with me, was it all OK? What about that weird smile? I dunno, when I first got there it was like she was pulling away, which was strange. It was like I'd overstepped some mark. It was dead confusing and I didn't feel good, so I turned my music right up. Loud. Trying to drown out my thoughts.

But even over the noise I could hear shouting. It was coming from outside, or was it downstairs? Someone was banging on my door. Bourgeois fucks probably wanted me to turn the music down.

"Leave me alone!" I yelled, but whoever was at the door was too stupid to understand.

I threw the door open. "Just leave me alone, yeah?"

It was Sam from upstairs, and he looked well scared. "Karo, it's the fash!" He legged off down the hallway.

I looked out the window, and there they were, a mob of skins heading up Thaerstrasse. Coming for us.

I ran down the stairs after Sam. Housemates were at the front door, pushing whatever they could find against it: beds, cupboards, bits of wood. I looked in the ground floor flat, the shutters had been let down, and mattresses were being pushed against the windows. Into the kitchen, Schimmel was there, on the CB, trying to get a response.

"Thaeri, this is Thaeri. We need help. Fascist attack! Help! Is anyone there? Anyone?"

Shit, no-one was monitoring the radios. We thought we'd dealt with the fash, we'd relaxed—and now we were going to pay the price.

"Help! This is Thaeri—anyone? Please!"

Schimmel was sweating, his eyes were wide open and he was frantically twisting knobs.

"Help! Fash attack! Help! This is Thaeri, anyone receiving?"

There was a stir, a voice hissing over the little speaker. That wasn't the main Friedrichshain station at the *Schreina*, it was from further away, maybe it wasn't even meant for us.

Schimmel calmed down a bit when he heard the voice, he fiddled with some dials, still talking into the mike. "Thaeri, this is Thaeri. Help, we need help, over."

"Kastanien, this is Kastanien. Thaeri do you read?"

Kastanien? That was all the way up in Prenzlauer Berg. The signal was indistinct, crackling and popping, but after Schimmel's fiddling we could just about make it out.

"Kastanien this is Thaeri. We read you. Fascist attack. Friedrichshain station not responding. Can you help? Over."

"Already on our way, hold tight!"

"Shit, Schimmel, what's happened to our station, why isn't anyone monitoring it?"

The first stones were already hitting the house, from the kitchen we could hear them rattling off the shutters, the glass splintering behind the mattresses.

"Prenzlauer Berg will be here soon, and they'll wake Friedrichshain up. I'll keep trying."

I left Schimmel at the radio and ran back to the front of the building. In the hall, there was a stream of people heading up the stairs, carrying crates and buckets of bottles, coal, cobblestones, anything they could lay their hands on.

"C'mon Karo, let's show the pricks what we're made of!"

We ran up the stairs: four landings, then a ladder to the roof. Five storeys below us about fifty skins were bunched up in front of our house. They had some kind of battering ram with them and were trying to break the door down.

"Fuck, there's more!" Sam was pointing at another bunch

of skins that were marching up the road. They were carrying black, red and yellow flags with the hammer and compass in the centre.

Kaminsky's gang.

DAY 5
Thursday
16th June 1994

We've all heard the news today, we know about the long queues on the border, the strict controls by the West Berlin and West German authorities. We've heard the West German Chancellor appeal for calm, and we've heard their excuses for closing the inner-German border.

They say they need to ensure the integrity of their borders. They talk about civil unrest in the GDR.

This is the talk of diplomats.

I am not a diplomat. I see a spade, I call it a spade; you know where you are with me.

So when I see our country in crisis, when I see our country brought to its knees by an incompetent leadership, I point the finger.

I point the finger at our weak government.

I point the finger at the unelected, anti-democratic Round Tables led by Hanna Krause. I point the finger at the saboteurs, the Round Tables interfering in the day to day running of our country. I point my finger and I say: enough!

Karo

It wasn't too bad. Not too much damage, thanks to the other squatters. They'd turned up just after Kaminsky's mob, coming from the other end of the street. The skins had taken one look and legged it. Sad fucks.

But at the meeting in the kitchen the next morning people were well pissed off. They were looking for someone to blame.

"It's your fault they targeted us!"

Everyone was staring at me. I didn't know if what they said was true or not, but what I did know was that some dick had sprayed *Republikschutz = Stasi pigs* on our door. And I was the only one who had anything to do with the RS.

"It's not my fault! They probably came for us because we're that bit further away from the other squats!"

"Yeah, well, they may be the fucking fash, but maybe they're right for once!"

"What the fuck? What are you talking about? Have you got any fucking idea what we do at RS? It's nothing like-"

"No better than the cops. You need to get your priorities straight, Karo."

"You know what, fuck the lot of you! At least I'm trying to do something for the revolution, not just sitting around feeling radical because I smoke spliff and drink beer all day!"

Fuck their stupid meeting, fuck their stupid collective house. I'd had enough. I went to my room and stuffed some clothes into a rucksack. No idea where I was going but I definitely wasn't going to stay here with these pseudo-punks.

When I picked up my bag and turned to the door Schimmel was there.

"Don't go, Karo. They're just scared, they don't mean it."

"Yeah well, nobody talks to me like that. Fuck the lot of them!"

"Karo, I've got to talk to you. About Becker."

I didn't say anything, just waited for Schimmel to say what he had to say.

"Look, Karo, I really appreciate it, I mean, what you're doing. But ..."

"What? Just say it, Schimmel!"

"It's ... it's my problem. I appreciate what you've done, and why. But can you just leave it? It's me, I'm the one who's got to deal with it."

"You think I'm interfering? Is that it?"

I pushed past Schimmel and left the *Thaeri*. It'd been my home for nearly five years and now I was going. Fucking great week this was turning out to be!

I guess I wasn't that much different from all my housemates. I was pissed off and scared and I wanted to take it out on someone. When I left *Thaeri* I went round to the *Schreina* bar. Antifa Bert was there, as I'd expected, but the door was locked and I had to knock to be let in. When Bert opened up I was fair, I didn't lay into him immediately. I gave him a chance.

"Hi Bert. Just wondering, who was monitoring the CB last night?"

At least he had enough self-awareness to look embarrassed.

"Karo, look, I'm sorry, I had to go out—it was just for a few minutes." That was a first, I'd never heard Bert apologise to anyone for anything. But this time he'd fucked up. Big time.

"So you heard about what happened then? Didn't see you coming to help."

"Someone had to stay here, keep an eye on the radios, just in case, you know ..."

"And wasn't it you who said we could stop monitoring the radios? We don't need to worry about the skins any more, you said, because your friend Kaminsky's tamed them. Well guess what—a load of Kaminsky's lads were there last night!"

"No, can't be. That wouldn't have happened. Couldn't have been them, someone else, stirring up trouble-"

"Fuck's sake, Bert, I saw the same fucking mob at Kaminsky's demo earlier on!"

He was still shaking his head, didn't want to believe it.

"You need to get your priorities straight, Bert." I admit I stole that line from my housemates. *Ex*-housemates. "Because if you don't sort yourself out then I for one won't want to work with you!"

"Fuck you, Karo, you sanctimonious shit! At least I'm not working for the cops!"

12:01
Karo

After the shit morning I'd just had I jumped at the chance of meeting up with Katrin—she was exactly the person I needed right then. She'd left a message for me at work, saying she could miss a lecture, did we want to meet up? It was the first time she'd suggested we do something—until now it had been me doing all the running.

"I'm so glad you're here," I told her.

We were lying on the grass in Treptower Park, Katrin's t-shirt had ridden up, leaving her belly bare to the sunlight. Her skin was literally glowing and all I wanted to do was snuggle up to her, kiss that golden tummy.

"No worries. I heard about the new border controls and decided I should come over. It's easier for me to cross the Wall—they're not hassling Westerners."

"Are you a *Wessi* now?" I'd aimed for teasing, but Katrin just shrugged and turned her head to one side. I tried a different tone: "I'm glad you made a bit of time for us."

"Well don't get used to it, It's not often I have cancelled lectures," Katrin mumbled.

"But I *want* to get used to this!" My hand edged up

Katrin's flank.

Somehow that didn't please her—she flinched, just a teeny bit, but I could feel it.

"What's up?"

Katrin was now sitting up, she was looking off into the distance, her hair curtaining her face. "It's just, well, you know I don't have much time. I need to get a move on with my studies, I have to fit in a few more seminars ..."

"That's OK, I can work around that. Whenever you want me-"

"Karo," Katrin turned to look at me. She was using a serious voice, her face told me she was determined to say whatever it was she had to say. "Look, I don't think, you know, at the moment ..."

"You don't want to see me any more? Is that was this is?"

"Oh, Karo, don't go off on one, I'm just trying to-"

"I'm not going off on one!"

There was no response. I was glaring around the park, but still watching her out of the corner of my eye. She was picking random pieces of grass and stripping them, looking worried. My mind was churning, trying to come up with explanations for her behaviour.

"You said you'd be there, that you'd be there for me!"

"Karo, I am! I'm right here."

"It doesn't feel like it at the moment, it feels like you're saying you don't want to see me any more-"

"I'm just saying I think we should take this a bit more slowly."

I didn't answer, just grabbed my stuff and headed off.

"Karo, wait!"

But I didn't wait, Katrin had made clear what she wanted, and it wasn't me.

Martin

I don't know what time it was when they came, so little light filtered through the holes in the steel window that I couldn't say whether it was still early or already midday.

The door banged open to reveal two men. I don't think they were the same ones as before, but they could have been: same build, same clothing, same silence. One had an unlit cigarette in his hand.

"Can I have some water?"

They didn't answer, just stood by the door, one to either side of the frame. I got the hint and walked out of the cell, following one of the men down the corridor while the other brought up the rear.

I was ushered into a room. This one had a window, a table and two chairs. I sat myself on one of the chairs, turning to ask again for water. But the men had gone and the door was shut.

This place also felt familiar, it stood in for all the interrogation rooms I've ever been in. I knew the drill. They'd keep me waiting here for a while, then someone would come in, probably holding a cup of tea or some other beverage, and they'd be only too willing to get me a drink, but first a quick chat …

Even though I knew how it worked I couldn't stop thinking about my dry throat. They'd kept me in a hot cell overnight and not given me anything to drink. My head was throbbing, as bad as any hangover. I sucked my teeth, trying to muster some saliva but nothing came.

The door opened again and a soldier appeared. British Army fatigues. Some kind of junior officer, just the one set of pips.

"Good morning, my name is Sanders." He shook my hand and gave me an absent smile.

"I'd like some water." We were speaking German, which

made me feel a little more confident.

"What? Oh, of course. Certainly."

The captain set a pile of files down, then went back to the door. He opened it a fraction and, in English, ordered a bottle of water.

"Now where were we?" The officer sat down opposite me and busied himself with looking through his files. He had a pair of half-moon glasses perched on the end of his nose, he was squinting through them as he turned the pages.

"I'm not going to answer any questions until you give me something to drink."

He looked up, his wide eyebrows raised, making his forehead crinkle.

"You've kept me in a cell overnight with nothing to drink, and you haven't told me why I'm being held."

"I say, old chap, we can't have that! But, rest assured, the water is on its way. And when we're done here I'll find out who's responsible for this fiasco. You have my word on that."

"If it's all the same to you, I'd rather wait until the water gets here."

"Gosh, I'm awfully sorry about all of this. I quite understand your position, yes." Sanders closed the files, placing his glasses on top and clasping his hands in front of his belly, making him look just like a pastor at confirmation classes.

"I can only apologise, Mr ... er ..." Sanders moved his glasses and had a quick look at the first page of file in front of him. He was very quick about it, too quick, as if the files were empty. "I'm terribly sorry, I don't know your name."

"Grobe," I told him. "It says so in my *Ausweis*, which is in the bag you took off me yesterday."

"Well, Herr Grobe, there seems to have been some mix up, and if it were down to me I'd order you a taxi right away. Unfortunately for us, sir, once the army gets hold of you then there's all sorts of paperwork to wade through ... As I said, I can only apologise."

"So why are you holding me?"

"Well, yes, that's one of the things we need to get to the bottom of. I'm afraid I'll need your assistance in that matter. Just a few straightforward questions: what you're doing here in West Berlin, what exactly happened at the Prinzenbad, you know the kind of thing."

"I've already told you: not until I get some water."

Sanders' eyes flickered over my face.

"And once you get your glass of water, will you talk to us?"

I didn't bother answering, I put all my energy into staring back at this army officer.

He slipped a hand under the table, he made it look fairly natural, the way he slid his palm along the edge of the wood. But I was familiar with the gesture. A button had been pressed.

The door opened, and one of the guards came in. He set a bottle of water and a glass down in front of me.

"There we go," Sanders was wittering on in the background.

I reached for the water, already anticipating the hiss as I twisted the cap, the beads of carbon dioxide swimming up to the surface, the liquid pouring over my tongue, loosening my tight throat. Just as my hand closed around the bottle it was swiped out of my grasp. It skidded across the table, toppling over the edge and smashing on the floor.

I looked at the guard who had knocked the bottle, but he was standing to attention. Sanders moved towards the door.

"All yours, Sergeant," he said.

Sanders left the room and the sergeant took his seat. He leaned back, one hand stroking a tidy moustache under a nose that hooked to the right. Behind me I could feel the presence of another soldier.

"What were you doing in Kreuzberg yesterday?"

I didn't answer. In these situations it's much easier to keep absolutely quiet than try to stick to some kind of formula like 'no comment'. Once you open your mouth it's hard to shut it again—much better to keep it shut in the first place. It's something I should have remembered while Sanders was still here.

"Hard guy, are we? Well if you're that hard then you'll have heard about the Allied Occupation Rights. We're in Berlin, which is still under the administration of the Four Powers. And you Germans," the sergeant leaned in, his fingers dimpling the files left behind by Sanders, his face moving towards mine. "You Germans have no rights. Not a sodding one. We can keep you here for as long as we want, we can give you water or tea or bloody whisky if we choose. Or we can decide you get nothing. Entirely up to us." A smirk crept towards his moustache. "You. Have. No. Sodding. Rights. Capito?"

The whole charade wasn't impressing me. I'd been through worse. In the old days it was the Stasi, a few months ago the skinheads. The Stasi and the skins had told me they weren't ever going to let me go either, yet somehow I'd got through it all and out the other end.

I just wished he'd shut up and give me something to drink.

12:37

Karo

I wanted to go home, but I didn't have a home to go to. A small but loud part of me had hoped I could move in with Katrin, even though the idea was absurd. Even if she'd wanted me the border controls were too unpredictable to be commuting across the Wall every day.

But I couldn't stay here in the park surrounded by happy people doing happy people things in the sun. And I didn't want to cycle around aimlessly. I didn't want to do anything, I just wanted Katrin, but Katrin had rejected me, despite all her promises, despite the way I'd opened up to her, something I've never done with anyone else.

In the end I decided to go and see Martin, he was easy company and he was close to Katrin. It was as if by being with Martin I could somehow still be near Katrin, even though I knew it would hurt.

Romantic bullshit, I know, but that's what I was feeling right then.

So I went over to Martin's, and he wasn't there. I stood outside his door, fighting back tears, wondering what to do. I grabbed the pencil and the pad of paper that hung off his doorframe and wrote "FUCK YOU!!!!"

I ended up going back to the RS offices. There was nowhere else to go. I just sat in the stuffy office, drinking coffee, wondering what to do.

It didn't take long for Erika to come nosing round.

"Laura was looking for you before, but you'd gone out-"

"Yeah, had other stuff on, is that alright with you?"

Erika came in, holding both her hands up, palms out.

"I was just making conversation," she said.

"Yeah, well, next time you could try *Hi!* or even *How are you?*"

"So, Karo, *how are you*?"

I was blinking back tears by now and Erika came bustling over, she put her arms around me. It was what I needed, but it didn't help either because now I really was crying.

I told her about the fash attack last night, and the meeting at the *Thaeri* this morning. I didn't tell her about Schimmel giving me the brush off, or about breaking up with Katrin, if you can even call it breaking up because we never even had time to properly get together in the first place but now it was over before she'd even given us a chance ...

When the crying jag slowed Erika got up and made me another coffee.

"What about a pastry, or a bit of cake? I can pop down to the bakery-"

I shook my head. Coffee was enough right now.

"Where are you going to stay?"

"Dunno. I could go to one of the other squats, I suppose. But I need my own space, need a bit of time away from all that."

Erika nodded, cupping her hands around her coffee like you do on a cold day. There was a long silence.

"Look, Karo, you won't exactly have your own space, but if you want, then you can stay at mine for a bit. You'll be on the couch and-" She didn't manage to finish because I was giving her a big, tight hug.

11:30

Martin

The sergeant kept on and on at me. The same questions, again and again. *Why did you come to West Berlin? What were you doing yesterday? Who are you? Who did you meet at the swimming baths?*

I concentrated on the scarred the edge of the worn table, not even looking up when my interrogator slammed his palms down in front of me. *Don't say anything, concentrate on that mark on the table.* Even without the sergeant shouting in my ear I would have found it hard to concentrate, the dehydration was making me feel light-headed.

My interrogator was now marching around the room, moving a little closer to me with every circuit. At first, it was a whisper of air when he passed, now his foot caught my chair leg every circuit or so, sending a jolt through my body. Soon his hand would glance off my shoulder, or the back of my head. Casual, definitely-not-on-purpose, but calculated to crack my composure.

Not that I was composed. My tongue filled my mouth, my

brain was pushing against the inside of my skull, and my eyes were no longer able to focus on the table.

"Clarie." It was involuntary, like a prayer uttered at the moment of death.

My interrogator stopped his pacing. The silence was louder than all the shouting, the smacking of the table, the stomping around.

"What?"

I didn't answer. I wasn't even sure about what I'd just said, whether I'd even said it aloud.

The sergeant consulted his watch then went back to his side of the table, his hands sliding along the edge of the wood until his fingers caught on the button.

The liquid washed into my mouth, the bubbles of carbon-dioxide burning my cracked tongue. I drained the glass, the thirst smothering my body's need to breathe. The glass landed back on the table, my grip easing away, my chest heaving as my lungs sucked in air.

"*Noch eins.*"

The guard poured more water into the glass, watching impassively as I drank. Shorter sips this time, allowing the liquid to trickle into every corner of my mouth before it slid down my raw throat.

"Martin!" Clarie's voice. I didn't look up, still concentrating on the water. "Get out, you moron! And leave the bloody bottle where it is."

The guard scuttled off and Major Clarie set the bottle of water back down on the table, next to me.

"I came as soon as I heard, how long have these buffoons had you in their tawdry mitts? Appalling, absolutely appalling, I can't apologise enough."

"More water."

Clarie opened the door. "Water, get some more water. Bring a crate of the damned stuff. And tea!"

I was feeling more human now, my head still throbbed, but my tongue was already shrinking to its normal size. I could only put Clarie off for a few more minutes, I had to use what time I had to get some answers ready.

"Right, let's get all this ironed out." Clarie was speaking his own brand of German: plum-in-the-throat accent, strange idioms: *Das werden wir gleich ausgebügelt kriegen.*

A crate of water bottles arrived, and a pot of tea with two cups and saucers, sugar and milk. How did they brew tea so quickly? Did they have it on tap, like the Russians with their samovars?

Clarie ignored the soldier who brought the drinks, using the time to look me over.

"Play mother, shall I?" He'd lost me: *Mutter spielen*? What was he talking about?

"Martin, you must accept my apologies," he said as he poured tea into the cups. "Seems to have been a bit of a mix up, actually."

"If you wanted to talk then all you had to do was give me a ring." I was feeling safer now, I allowed myself some indignation.

"Yes, well, it's a little more delicate than that, as I'm sure you'll appreciate. Sugar? Yes, you'll take a bit of sugar." I watched the major stir three teaspoons into my tea, followed by milk. "You see, your reasons for being at that swimming pool, not entirely above board, what?"

My mind went back to the Kaisers bag the source had been left by my side. Why would the Brits be interested in it?

"You see, we were expecting someone else. My men couldn't show you their accreditation because of the Americans. We can't afford to upset the Cousins, can we now?" Kreuzberg is in the American zone, so presumably Major Clarie had no business kidnapping East Germans there.

"So what do you want?"

"A person of interest. We were actually following him—not you. Although I must say we seem to have lost track of his-nibs, anyway, it seems his-nibs made a pass at you in the baths. Naturally that aroused the curiosity of my men. Good men, by the way, the best. A tad enthusiastic, now and again." Clarie took a sip of his tea. "Rather unfortunate that no-one realised it was you we had in the bag, so to say." Clarie chuckled but continued talking when I didn't join in. "You really should have asked for me earlier, could have had this all sorted out in a jiffy."

"What's your interest?"

"Same as yours, I imagine." Clarie was looking over the rim of his teacup. "Your contact—I'm told he's a good pal of Dr. Kaminsky."

They gave me my bag back and the use of a driver. I couldn't tell whether my driver was one of the goons who had arrested me, he looked similar, but didn't they all?

We drove for quite a while in the unmarked car, heading first back to Kreuzberg, then taking one of the main roads that led out of Hermannplatz. After that I was in parts of Berlin I'd never seen. I asked which Border Crossing Point I was being taken to.

"Sonnenallee, sir. Much quieter than the border posts in the city centre. Easier to make sure you won't be checked so thoroughly there."

Not being thoroughly checked sounded good to me, I'd rather avoid the attentions of the West Berlin police.

Traffic had thinned by now, other than a row of double-decker yellow buses we were the only vehicle on the road. We turned off onto a side street and parked outside some concrete flats that would have looked at home on either side of the Wall.

"Just go through the checkpoint, after that it's another three hundred metres to the bus stop. Good luck, sir."

I got out of the car, and looked back at the main road we'd just turned off. A long, brown hut presumably housed West Berlin customs and police. In front of that, next to a gap in the Wall, a solitary West Berlin policeman leaned on a railing. A watchtower presided over the crossing point.

I walked up to the cop, trying to look natural, trying not to think of the border controls on the S-Bahn last Tuesday.

The policeman had straightened up at my approach, moving away from the railing and into the middle of the road.

"*Ihren Ausweis, bitte.*"

I handed over my papers, and the cop flicked through them, not really paying attention.

"Going home?" he asked.

I wasn't sure whether he was trying to make small talk, or whether the question was the prelude for yet another interrogation. Either way, I was too nervous to answer, so I nodded.

The policeman handed my papers back to me and waved me on. A few paces later, I was through the gap in the Wall, and the East Berlin border guard was giving me a lazy salute. But I hadn't quite made it yet—this was one of the original crossing points, built before the Wall opened up: I had to pass through five gates and walls in the compound. Cars that were making the journey from East to West had a two-hundred metre slalom to negotiate, zig-zagging around bollards and staggered openings between intermediary walls.

There was no challenge as I passed the final barracks, the final watchtower and the final gate.

I was home. I was back in East Berlin.

Karo

I left soon after that cup of coffee with Erika. There was no point being in the office, and I'd decided to go round to Martin's again: I felt guilty about that nasty note I'd left. It hadn't been fair—it wasn't his fault that he'd not been at home when I needed him. I shouldn't take my shit out on him.

When I got to Martin's I checked the notebook. The page I'd written on had been torn out, but I could still trace the words FUCK YOU!!!! scored into the surface of the next sheet. I pressed Martin's bell, wondering how he'd react when he saw me.

I got a bit of a shock when he opened up. He looked like shit. His clothes were crumpled and there was a gross, sour smell coming off him.

"Karo."

"Well don't sound sooo pleased to see me!" Then again, considering the note I'd left him earlier ... I took a step back, both in my head and in real life. "I'm sorry about the note-"

"What do you want?" Martin was still standing in the doorway, he hadn't invited me in.

"You OK, Martin? You look even worse than last time I saw you."

"Bit tired, Karo. Maybe another time?"

"If there's anything you need ..."

"I'll let you know." Martin shut the door.

OK, I got it, Martin was pissed off with me because I'd left him a note saying *fuck you*. Or was there something else? I mean, how many times have I left him messages this last week, and did he ever get back to me? What was going on? Had he heard about my trip to the Party archives? Or about me and Katrin?

Whatever was bothering Martin, he didn't look good. He looked like he'd been sleeping in his clothes, he smelled like he hadn't washed for days, and I definitely got a whiff of schnapps on his breath.

I wasn't the only one needing a bit of help.

Martin

After I got rid of Karo I had a shower and thought about going to bed for a bit, catch up on some sleep. But I knew I'd lie there, wondering what was in that Kaisers carrier bag. I still hadn't looked, until now I hadn't even had the energy to be curious, but maybe it was time to open up the bag, see if there was anything useful.

When I got to the Stralau office I spread the contents of the plastic bag over my desk. Lots of documents to do with Kaminsky's rally on Saturday: situation reports, summaries, assessments, developmental reports, departmental reports, information for the ministerial committee, for *Volkspolizei* departmental heads. I had a pile of paper about ten centimetres high, all recording concerns, worries, fears for Kaminsky's well-being on the day, along with plans of how to keep him safe. I had no way of knowing if this was the usual bureaucratic headless-chicken act, whether this level of concern was normal or represented a heightened state of alert. I needed Steinlein's expertise.

In the absence of my partner I tried to summarise for myself what I had here. A collection of police reports, all concentrating on Kaminsky and his big rally. Public order planning, plans for the deployment of the Red Cross of the GDR, public transport logistics and all the other things that need to be organised for a mass mobilisation.

Other documents focussed on assessing and providing for potential risks to the safety of the speakers before, during and after the rally.

Looking at the circulation lists attached to the front of

these documents I could see that most of them had also been distributed to Kaminsky's office. Other names that came up regularly were the President of the *Volkspolizei*, the police minister, the Committee of the Ministry of Internal Affairs, and Captain Neumann of Lichtenberg K1.

But what I found most significant was the fact that our source had provided only files relating to the rally in Treptower Park. Why no information on other appearances on Kaminsky's barnstorming tour? He'd been travelling the country, holding rallies and demonstrations regularly. This rally in Treptower Park was planned to be the biggest one, marking the end of Kaminsky's first stage of campaigning before the *Volkskammer* elections, but that didn't explain why I'd only been given the files for this one event.

Our source was telling us something. Our source was telling us that the assassination attempt on Kaminsky would happen in just two days.

15:14
Martin

I heard the front door slam shut, followed by Steinlein's cane drumming up the stairs.

"Where have you been? I waited for you all night!" He stood in the doorway, jaw clenched, hands on hips, playing the disciplinarian father.

I held out a few sheets from the papers I'd brought back from West Berlin and Steinlein closed in for a look. Jamming his cane under his elbow, he took the proffered sheets. "What happened?"

"British intelligence pulled me in. Kept me overnight."

"British intelligence?" Steinlein's eyes were buried deep below his brow, darkness directed at me. "What did you tell them?"

"They were following the person who had this bag," I gestured to the carrier bag, still half full of reports. "When he passed it to me the Brits decided they'd like a chat."

"What did you tell them? Did they see these?" Steinlein's cane swung into the pile of papers, flattening them against the desk.

"A few hours of interrogation. Nothing too bad, just the kind of thing you've probably done yourself a few times. I didn't tell them anything."

"And the files?"

"Of course they've looked at the bloody files, what do you think?"

"You should have stopped them!" Steinlein's cane swooped again and the papers flitted through the air, spilling over the floor.

I left him to his tantrum and went over to the kitchen-niche. While the water was boiling I watched Steinlein awkwardly stoop down, using the head of his cane to gather in the loose leaves.

"Is this what the source gave you? This is dynamite!" Steinlein had regained a measure of his former calm, but he was still gripping the walking stick so tightly that his knuckles were white. "What did he say? Did he tell you anything useful?"

"He didn't say anything—I didn't see him."

Steinlein was hardly listening, he was sitting at the desk now, carefully turning over each sheet, scanning the text as he went. "This is an impressive haul."

"Any theories on how he managed to get hold of these files?"

"Heaven knows, but it's pretty extensive." Steinlein pushed his chair back and stretched, a sheet of paper in one hand. "Look, there's another note from our source: *Use Tacheles dead drop to contact.* At least now we know how to get hold of him."

I looked at the writing Steinlein had found—same as last time, vague pencil marks between the lines of a report. How did Steinlein find these messages?

"I've got some more good news," he said, his voice softening still further, the ghost of a smile beginning to tease his lips. "The officer responsible for securing the outer perimeter of Kaminsky's next rally has fallen ill, I'm taking over his squad. I'll be on the inside, I'll have access to collateral and can corroborate at least some of this material. Might even give us a clue who our informant is."

"Why are you a cop?"

Steinlein stopped rustling through the reports, the sudden change of subject confusing him.

"What do you mean?"

"Just curious. I still don't understand why you're doing all this." I looked around the office, taking in the scope of the investigation that Steinlein had kicked off. But it was really the same question that I had asked the other night: was Steinlein doing this for Kaminsky, or because preventing crime was his job?

"I told you, I'm a police officer. This is what I do."

"But why?"

Steinlein took a roll of parchment paper from his bag and limped over to the wall. He unrolled the sheet, tacking the upper corners to the wall. It was a blueprint of the area around the Soviet War Memorial in Treptower Park.

I waited patiently as he smoothed the plans out and tacked a bottom corner down. Eventually he spoke, his back still turned to me.

"My father was a builder, he headed up the construction and maintenance brigade on an LPG farm in the Uckermark. The whole brigade had this racket going, they'd steal building materials and sell it on to people building their *Datsche* and weekend cottages."

"And that bothered you?"

"At home he was a real stickler for discipline. He'd get drunk every Saturday night then come home and beat me and my brother for the week's transgressions. Once he beat us for scrumping apples from a neighbour's tree. Kids are sensitive to hypocrisy and injustice, and when he beat me that time it was like a switch had flicked. I hit him back." Steinlein pushed the last drawing pin in.

"And that's why you became a cop?"

"I told the Party Organisation at the farm about my father's activities." Steinlein took a step back to admire his handiwork. "Nothing happened—he was too well-connected. There might have been an internal Party disciplinary hearing, but if so then nothing came of it. It's no surprise the Party collapsed in 1989; it was high time for change. Internal renewal.

"Anyway, when I informed on my father he made me leave home. I signed up for three years in the army, after that: officer career path in the *Volkspolizei*."

Steinlein limped back to the desk and sat down. He didn't say anything else, just concentrated on his file.

We were looking through the paperwork again, comparing notes. It bothered me that we didn't know who the source was.

"The person who gave me this bag is connected to Kaminsky. That's why British Defence Intelligence were interested in him." My words made Steinlein pause, his brow was furrowed, the eyes receding again under his stern brow. "I've been thinking about it all afternoon, I reckon our source-"

"Why are British intelligence interested in Kaminsky?" he interrupted.

"Clarie said he has to take a professional interest in what happens in East Berlin." I answered. "Called it his back-yard. Said it's his job to know if anyone's rocking the boat, and if so, how hard."

Steinlein pulled out a pack of f6 cigarettes and lit one,

looking up at the ceiling as he exhaled the first puff. "How does he know our source is connected to Kaminsky?"

"He didn't say. But who is our source? Is Clarie right about the Kaminsky connection? We should check out Kaminsky's staff and supporters—it's someone with access to the Stasi archives, that'll help narrow it down-"

"There's not enough time for all that." Steinlein waved a hand, dismissing the suggestion. "The rally is on Saturday and there are hundreds of people on his personal staff alone. Add all the Party apparatchiks he might be connected to ... What about your British major? Why don't we just ask him?"

"Clarie knows, but he won't tell me, not unless we can trade something, some intelligence he'd be interested in. That's the way he works."

Steinlein passed me the pack of cigarettes and his lighter.

"We haven't got anything for your Englishman, have we?" he asked while tapping the tip of his cigarette against the side of an aluminium ashtray. "Can we not persuade him it's in his interest to help us?"

Steinlein's questions had given me a new idea: Dmitri. "I could ask my FSK liaison. If Captain Pozdniakov knows anything he'll tell us."

"It's like talking to a brick wall!" Steinlein stabbed out his cigarette. "How many times do I have to say it? We can't let anyone know what we're doing here. No-one!"

"I don't see the problem, if Clarie knows about it then surely we can talk to the Friends-"

"The Friends? Talking to the Friends went out of fashion with *Perestroika*! We can't trust the Russians, they're too close to the Party!" Steinlein went to the window, leaning his forehead against the glass. "There's no way you're talking to your Russian. There's too much at stake, and that's final!"

Martin

As I entered the office, Dmitri hastily shut the file on his desk, turning it over so the front cover wasn't visible. He looked up and a smile split his face when he saw it was me.

"Martin Ottovich! Good, good that you are here my friend —you are looking better. Recovering from your adventures, I am glad to see."

Except I wasn't looking better, I knew that. I was knackered and strung out. Dmitri came out from behind his desk and gave me a slap on the shoulder. Turning to a filing cabinet he retrieved a bottle of vodka and two glasses.

Before he could place the glasses on his desk there was a knock and his assistant came halfway into the room, speaking in a low voice, speaking in Russian.

Dmitri turned to me, his face grave. "My friend, do you know you were followed here?" He saw my reaction and asked. "What is your reason to visit today?"

"Kaminsky. We were wondering whether you-"

Dmitri put the glasses and bottle down then reached for the door handle. "Martin, leave at once. If anyone asks, say you came to visit me, to drink a toast for old time's sake. Tell them I was not here when you came. So you leave without seeing me." The Russian officer opened the door wide, the remarkable force of his personality was distilled into that one action, impelling me into the corridor. "1800 hours. Be at the Fauler See in Weissensee—you know it? There's a bench at the east side of the lake. Wait no more than fifteen minutes. Now go!"

Martin

My watch told me it was exactly six. I was on the bench in the woods that surround the stagnant puddle they call the Fauler See. There was nobody around, nothing to be heard in the still heat of the afternoon. For ten minutes I watched the vague reflections of the still reeds on the scummy water. It was hard not to doze off in the sharp scent of the pines.

I heard wheezing and the rustle of dederon long before the old man stumbled into view, leaning heavily on a crutch. He slumped down next to me, and, still gasping for breath, pushed a filterless cigarette between his lips. He lit up and inhaled deeply.

I wondered whether the old man had been sent by Dmitri. If he wasn't one of Dmitri's then I was in trouble—he looked like a talker and while he was here my contact wouldn't approach. But I was wrong, the man sitting next to me didn't say a word, just sucked heavily on his cigarette. When his cigarette was exhausted, he pulled out another and lit up, dropping the packet on the bench between us as he began to cough. He hawked up a mouthful of tanned phlegm, spitting onto the marshy ground, and in the same moment flicked the packet of cigarettes towards me. Without thinking, I placed my hand over it as the smoker got up. He nodded to me and dragged himself off down the path, cigarette dangling from his lips.

I waited until he was out of sight before leaving the bench. It was now a quarter past six, I'd been here for exactly fifteen minutes.

The path meandered around trees and bushes and I waited until I was between two bends before checking the cigarette packet. It had been emptied of cigarettes, but nestling between lining and carton was a cigarette paper, the kind used for rolling tobacco. I took it out and unfolded it, squinting to read the cramped handwriting.

70 → Zingsterstr
Alight Ribnitzer Str
S-Bahn 1st carriage → H-schönh
Steps to bridge
58, 2nd carriage → M-E-Platz
S-Bahn → Alex
Centrum menswear

I headed out of the woods, back into the baked fetor of civilisation, jogging the last few metres to meet the tram that was already shuffling around the corner.

I boarded and stamped my ticket, casting an eye over the other passengers. The smoker had passed me a dry cleaning list, a zig-zag course through Berlin that would hopefully show up any tail I might have. Dmitri would have one of his spooks shadowing me, keeping an eye out for any other followers—all I had to do was play the game, work through the list until I got to the menswear department of the Centrum store on Alexanderplatz.

Fifteen minutes later I got off and walked down the canyon of new-build flats, using plate glass shop windows and the side mirrors of parked cars to keep an eye on anyone coming up behind. The few people who had got off the tram with me were quickly swallowed up in the concrete labyrinth of Hohenschönhausen.

Even though I knew Dmitri would have people watching my back I was sensitive to my surroundings. As I stopped to buy an unnecessary ticket at the station, a man in a white shirt with a sparse purple paisley pattern, dark blue corduroy trousers and straw hat walked past me. I pushed my 20 Pfennig coin into the machine and watched the man go up the steps to the platform, unable to shake a feeling of familiarity.

I took my ticket and followed the man up to the platform. He was walking up and down, a lit cigarette cupped in his hand.

The train whined in and I got in the first carriage. The man in the paisley shirt flipped his cigarette into the gap between train and platform edge and entered through the same door. Our eyes met as he looked around for a seat, and instead of glancing away I held his eyes for the half-second or so before he moved his gaze.

I kept Paisley Shirt in my sights, watching his reflection in the window, wondering whether he'd try to stop me leaving the train. I could feel sweat trickling down the back of my neck, sliding under my collar, making it damp. The windows were open, the wheels clacked loudly along the track, a beat that gave rhythm to my thoughts. I had to get away from this man. I had to lose him when I got off at the next stop. He was young, wiry, he could easily outrun me. Did Dmitri have anyone nearby, had they already picked up my trail? Could I rely on them to take out Paisley Shirt?

Using the reflections in the window I checked the other occupants of the carriage, hoping I would recognise somebody as being associated with Dmitri. I could see two young women at the end of the carriage, laughing at the antics of a small child in a pushchair. No help to be expected from that direction, I was on my own.

The next station was already drawing near, the train slowing, the sound of the wheels deepening and slackening. I had to time my next movements exactly, if I were even a couple of seconds out, my plan would fail. In my head I measured the distance to the doors, calculated how long it would take to unpeel myself from the sticky vinyl seat. We were on one of the new red and grey S-Bahn trains, doors operated by push-button. Once the doors were closed they couldn't be hauled open again. That was my chance.

I stayed in my seat as we pulled into the next station. Adrenaline pumped through my body, I had to make a real effort to remain where I was, peering through the dusty window. The platform was empty, and the tannoys almost immediately crackled, coughing commands to stay back: *Zurückbleiben*. On the train the red light glowed, the signal sounded *Tu-tüüü-tu*.

I jumped up, jamming my hand between the closing doors, pushing against them, slipping through the gap.

"*Zurückbleiben!*" the tannoys yelled as I landed on the platform. I turned, facing the train. Paisley shirt was no longer in his seat, he was pinned against a partition, his arm pulled high up his back by one of the women.

As the train pulled out of the station the mother met my eye. She winked.

A tram, then another S-Bahn took me to Alexanderplatz station. It was hotter in the centre of the city, and I was glad to enter the relative cool of the Centrum department store. I climbed the steps to the fourth floor, checking for any tail at each landing, then pretended to admire the meagre offerings in the men's department.

After a minute or so a member of staff announced the store was closing. He came closer, as if to flush out any errant shoppers from between the aisles.

Even though menswear was empty he whispered, using the corner of his mouth to mutter the words as he sidled past, *Emergency exit, then stairs to roof.*

I followed the signs to the fire exit, first up some concrete steps, then climbing a rusty steel ladder, before pushing at the steel hatch above. It opened easily, and I climbed out, lowering the hatch back into place.

"Martin, glad you could make it!" Dmitri was standing behind the hatch, looking comfortable despite the heat. He was no longer in uniform but wore East German clothes: light shirt, grey trousers and brown closed sandals. A warm breeze made its way across the open rooftop. There was no shelter up here, it was obvious we were alone.

"So, you've been caught up in the Kaminsky situation? What's the interest?"

"There's a plot to assassinate Kaminsky, we're trying to find out more. We have a source, we don't know who it is, but British Defence Intelligence might."

"Assassinate Kaminsky?" Dmitri chuckled. "Are you not tempted to let them get on with it? No, no, a small joke. I understand your concern. So, DIS are interested in your informant? Are they aware that he is working for you?" Dmitri's one good eye was dancing, he was having his fun with me, for all the seriousness of the matter. "Maybe your informant is actually working for the Queen, perhaps the product comes directly from Major Clarie?"

I considered this for a moment. It seemed possible, but not likely. Why would the British want to feed us information? Or disinformation? The whole situation simply felt improbable, and that was perhaps why I was feeling so lost.

"You'd better give me the whole story, my friend. Start at the beginning."

I told Dmitri what I knew. There wasn't much to tell; for me it had all begun less than a week ago. Dmitri listened without interrupting, but I could see he was making his usual mental notes.

"So you are working with Lieutenant Steinlein. The name is familiar, who is he exactly? And why are you not working with your team at RS?"

"Steinlein is uniformed *Volkspolizei*, but he's seconded to the political policing unit, K1. He was hospitalised by the fascists a few days before they got hold of me."

"Let me guess—he used this fact to build a bridge to you? Something you have in common, being attacked by skinheads?" Dmitri smiled as I nodded my head. "And your colleagues at RS?"

"Steinlein is insisting on secrecy. He says he doesn't know who to trust."

"Does he suggest your colleagues may be part of this plot?"

"He suspects the Ministry and the police. He seems very worried, sees a conspiracy wherever he looks."

"Does he know we are meeting? No? Very good. Tell me, are no alarm bells ringing in that head of yours?" Dmitri lit one of his black cigarettes. "No, of course not, ever the trusting Martin."

"I haven't any energy for alarm bells. I haven't the energy to deal with this shit, not today, not ever," I replied. "Kaminsky wants to destroy what we've created. And right now he's succeeding. Everything we stand for, everything we ever fought for—if Kaminsky has his way, all that effort will have been wasted."

Dmitri let me ramble, pulling on his cigarette, looking up at the Television Tower that loured over the railway station opposite.

"Somehow, back in 1989, the revolution started, the Party fell, people wanted change, and together we made that change happen.

"But now I'm wondering whether people really *wanted* change. Because as soon as Kaminsky crawls out of the ruins of the Party ... it's like he's the answer to everyone's prayers."

Dmitri didn't answer immediately, instead leading me to the edge of the roof. Seven storeys below us, Alexanderplatz was crowded with shoppers, ants negotiating their way around each other, dividing and clumping together again.

"Martin, you're tired. But are you not also apprehensive about the future? For years you've been thinking about all of this, imagining and discussing different ways of organising society. Yet still you're afraid. How do you think all of those people down there feel? They want to be reassured, they want to know what's going to happen next. As a nation you're feeling your way. You want people to be responsible for their own lives and communities, but is that what *they* want? They've always been told what to do. They've always known what was acceptable and what would bring them trouble and grief. Why shouldn't they want a return to simpler times? Times when they felt they had control over at least the immediate aspects of their lives.

"With your revolution you are offering people freedom. Freedom to take on the responsibility for running society. Freedom to negotiate with their co-workers, their neighbours, their city, their country. They are able to take part in the constant dialogue that is freedom at a societal level. But when there's a fair dialogue no-one knows the outcome, there is no way of predicting the results. Not knowing how things will turn out is scary. Don't underestimate the power of fear. And don't underestimate the power held by those who say they can take fear away."

The smoke from Dmitri's cigarette hung in the air between us as we watched at the masses below. "Freedom is change," he said to the shimmering skyline. "Freedom is danger. Freedom is insecurity." Dmitri dropped his cigarette onto the cement roof, carefully grinding it out with his sandal. "Not everyone wants that. To them Kaminsky offers simple answers, a return to simpler times. He offers to remove the burdens of thinking and doing. He offers a return to the old days."

DAY 6
Friday
17th June 1994

Over the last few days many people have come up to me in the street, they're upset, angry about the delays at the border. They're asking me: do I condemn West Germany for causing these problems?

Let me be completely clear about this: nobody condemns the West German border controls as strongly as I.

The West Germans can talk all they like about 'continued unrest'. They can prattle on about 'protecting' their borders—but at the end of the day it is normal people who are suffering.

It's people like you and me, people like your family, your friends and your workmates. We are the ones suffering from these new controls imposed by the West.

But when it comes to trade, it's business as usual. When it comes to Bonzen *crossing the border, it's business as usual. The political elite have no trouble with crossing into West Berlin—for them the borders remain open.*

But if you or I want to visit friends or family in the West we are treated very differently. We have to put up with strict border controls: long waits, searches and questioning.

Can we expect the government to do anything about this?

Of course not.

Karo

Erika dragged me into the office with her this morning, which meant I got there ultra-early, like before I was even properly awake. When Laura saw me she was absolutely merciless.

"Since we're all here can we start our meeting?"

So basically I wasn't all there for the morning meeting. I don't think they talked about anything important, it sounded like updates and divvying up tasks. Afterwards I was heading back to my own office for a snooze when Laura stopped me.

"Any luck in your efforts to track down Dr. Becker?"

"I've got an address for him, but that's from 1988. I tried phoning but the line was dead. I guess he doesn't live there any more."

"A lot of people have moved around since the start of the revolution. Have you checked the address registration files at the police station? Although, that may be a little direct—you don't want to set too many alarm bells ringing, do you? But, chin up, I may have something of use."

Brilliant! Knowing Laura she'll have some kind of secret index, compiled by hand using old Stasi files and informants' reports! I followed her into the front office, starting to feel a bit hopeful again.

"Grit, could you pass me the telephone directory for Berlin, please?" Laura asked the secretary.

"A *phone* book?"

"Don't sound so puzzled—your Dr. Becker is likely to have a phone, a man with his connections."

She was right. I took the phone book from Grit and headed back to my office.

Once there I opened the book at B and scanned through until I got to Becker. There was no Dr. Becker, just lots of Beckers with their initials. In fact about thirty Beckers with the initial A were listed. Thirty! What was I meant to do, phone every single one of them up? *Excuse me, sorry to bother you, but are you the bastard who hurt my friend about five years ago?*

Erika came in, saw me with my head in my hands and said: "Phone book no good then?"

"Are you checking up on me again?"

"Yes." She said it in such a matter of fact way that I couldn't feel pissed off with her. She knew things weren't going too well in my life right now, apart from obviously being homeless, but she didn't push me to tell her anything. She just made sure I knew she was available if I did want to talk. I appreciated that.

She went over to Martin's desk and poked around a bit. "It's always surprised me how messy Martin is."

"Yeah, he's got some Neues Deutschland over there—from 1987! Ancient!"

Erika found the Party newspapers and laughed at the headlines. "Look at this: *Farmers keep their word and deliver bumper crop*—that's the headline! They didn't believe in giving us any real news back then. *Greetings to the Democratic People's Party of Afghanistan. The Central Committee wishes the 2nd National Conference every success.*"

Erika was flicking through the paper, laughing at the stuffy stories when suddenly she stopped her rustling and giggling.

"Karo, you should take a look at this."

I peered over her shoulder at the article she'd found.

New deputy director for youth facility. Scanning through all the ridiculous titles and empty phrases that clogged up the first paragraph, I got to the interesting bit: *The Ministry for People's Education has appointed Herr Dr. Andreas Becker, resident in Strausberg, as new deputy director of the Berlin* Durchgangsheim.

"That's him, that's the fucker!" I double-checked my notes,

yes, October 1987.

"So now you know that he used to live in Strausberg. Maybe he moved back later?"

"Grit!" I shouted through the open office door. "Have we got the phone book for the Frankfurt District?"

"Ask at the post office."

08:20
Karo

I had to queue for what felt like hours at the post office, stuck in a huddle of sweaty, smelly Berliners. If anything makes you want to stop believing in humanity then it's queuing in a government department during a heat wave.

Most people were discussing the rumours about Hanna Krause, the chair of the Central Round Table. She was going to be at Kaminsky's rally the next day. Nobody knew what was going on, whether there'd been some kind of deal. Whatever it was, it must be mega, just look at the way Kaminsky had been slagging Hanna Krause off, saying she was hysterical and calling the Round Tables *knitting circles of saboteurs* (he obviously doesn't realise just how dangerous knitting circles can be).

It just didn't make any sense, didn't tie in with the stories Erika had told me about what Hanna used to get up to in the old days. People were coming up with fantastic conspiracy theories: *Kaminsky and Krause have fallen in love,* or *Krause's sold the Round Tables out.*

Listening to all that sick gossip put me in an even worse mood and when I finally got to the head of the queue the clerk behind the counter was really snotty with me. She sighed and complained about having to get off her arse to fetch the phone book.

"You know, you could just leave them out here in front. That way you could sit on your comfy seat all day long and not have to get up for people like me."

She gave me a look like she thought I was crazy. "These books are the property of the German Post, we can't just leave them lying around."

Honestly, sometimes I think these civil servants haven't even heard we're in the middle of a revolution.

The clerk came back and passed the Frankfurt district phone book over. "Move aside so that I can deal with other customers, and don't be too long about it."

I took the book to the tables they provide for you to fill in your withdrawal slips and customs declaration forms and stuff, and riffled through the pages until I got to the Beckers. I groaned, once again there was no Dr. Becker but there were about fifteen different A. Beckers. Great. I turned over a withdrawal slip and started to copy out the addresses and phone numbers, but sweat dripped off my forehead and splotched onto the rough paper. The damp patch kept growing, and was added to by another drop of sweat.

"Fuck it!" I said under my breath, and, checking nobody was watching, I tore out the page of Beckers and left the phone book on the table.

Back outside I considered my options. I could go back to the office, work through all these Beckers, try to eliminate them one by one, or I could do something less boring. The something less boring option was more than appealing right now—I was finding it hard to concentrate, every time I tried to do something my mind kept sliding off, towards Katrin or Schimmel or the *Thaeri*, or all of them bundled up together in a hard ball that sat in my stomach. I just ended up feeling sorry for myself, and that made me feel like a right sad case.

But I had a mission, and right now that mission was the only way I was managing to keep it together.

Karo

It felt like I'd spent the whole day getting hold of this list of phone numbers for A. Becker, but really it hadn't got me any further in my search. Then again, it hadn't really taken a whole day, it wasn't even midday and I'd done loads of other stuff too, like going up to the old Stasi HQ to look in the files there. I'd taken a list of made-up names so that it wouldn't be so obvious I was looking for that bastard Becker. Surprisingly, I drew a blank, which meant I had to spend a whole hour pretending to be interested in the records of these random people I'd never heard of. It was that bloody bureauctopus again: paperwork expanding to fill available sanity.

I was standing at the side of Frankfurter Allee, waiting for a gap in the traffic, when I had a thought. If Becker was involved in some fascist organisation then it was possible the police would have up-to-date files on him. I turned around and headed up the hill, towards Schottstrasse, the central police station in Lichtenberg. It was on the way up there that I remembered my horrendous experience at the Party archives on Tuesday. I decided to check in with Erika before I went barging in.

I found a phone box on Roedeliusplatz and dialled the RS number. "Erika, what would you say if I went to talk to the cops about Becker? I could say I was chasing Nazis."

There was the inevitable silence on the other end of the line while Erika thought about it.

"You'd need a good reason, but if you can think of one then why not? Tell them you're cross-referencing intelligence from a debriefing, make it from somewhere far away, the Mecklenburg coast or deepest Saxony."

"Yeah, and I could throw several names at them, not just Becker's." I was on top of this, I knew how to play this game now.

"Sounds good to me. But Karo?"

"Yeee-es?"

"Don't rub anyone up the wrong way. And if you meet a cop called Neumann, be careful. He's a nasty piece of work."

Neumann? I knew that name, Martin had mentioned him once. "Is he the one in political policing?"

"Yeah, K1. So if you're asking about Nazis then you'll probably run into him or one of his colleagues."

Oh, fun. Not only was I *voluntarily* going into a cop shop, but I was going to have to deal with fucking K1.

You know that feeling you get when a policeman looks at you, the feeling that you've done something wrong—even if you haven't? Well, that feeling is ten times worse when you actually go into a police station. It's that smell of disinfected fear—like at the dentist, but it's less physical, kind of deeper. Maybe you're a goody-two-shoes and have always seen the police as your friend and helper, maybe you didn't experience the police before 1989. But if you did, then you'll know what I'm talking about when I say I had *that* feeling.

I stood for absolutely ages at the front desk, while some jobsworth in a uniform pecked away at an electric typewriter.

"Oy! Some of us have got lives to get on with!" I shouted through the closed reception window.

The uniform hardly looked up, he'd clocked that I was a punk and was deliberately ignoring me.

I rapped on the partition, and pushed my RS pass up against the glass. "RS! Get your arse over here!"

Uniform got all interested all of a sudden. He scratched his head a bit then waddled over.

"You're from the RS?" He thought I was lying, I could tell he was thinking about booking me for impersonation.

"New times, everything's changing. Now tell me where to find Captain Neumann."

I followed the uniform's instructions, through doors and down corridors, and there he was: *Captain Neumann, Kriminalpolizei Department K1.* I knocked on the door next to the fancy name plate and went straight in.

Neumann turned out to be some kind of militarist doll come alive, complete with macho scar running down one side of his face. He was a bit surprised by a punk turning up in his office, I could tell because he raised an eyebrow half a millimetre.

"Captain Neumann, I'm Karo Rengold from RS2." I held my hand out. Not something I normally do for cops, and definitely not one from K1, but I wanted something from this bull and being polite was the easiest way to play it.

"Did we have an appointment, Fräulein Rengold?"

"It's *Frau* Rengold actually." God, what is it with these cops, don't they know it's the 1990s? "And no, we don't have an appointment, but don't worry—I'll be gone before you know it." I sat on a chair and plonked the list of names in front of him, the one I'd just used at the Stasi archive. "These are the names of people who may have had contact with the fascist house on Weitlingstrasse. I want to see their files."

Neumann picked up the list and read through the names. There was no eyebrow flickering this time, he was signalling that he'd never seen these names before.

"That can be arranged, Frau Rengold. When do you want them by?"

"As soon as possible. I was hoping to get a look at the first few right now."

Finally—a proper reaction! Neumann's mouth curved upwards, but just on one side. It was a dagger of a smile, a gloating curl of the lips. Not the kind of reaction I was aiming for.

"That won't be possible. As you may have heard there's a rally tomorrow, called by the General-Secretary of the PDS. We've got our hands a little full at the moment."

That was a crap excuse, and I told him so. The rally was in Treptow, but Schottstrasse was in the Lichtenberg district.

"Treptow police have requested our assistance in view of credible threats that have been made to the life of Dr. Kaminsky."

"OK, Monday then?" There was not a lot else I could say, the man had already said no.

"Monday then, Fräulein Rengold," he said as he handed me my list.

11:00
Martin

The Treptower Park meadows were full of sunbathers, walkers and volleyball players enjoying the sunshine. I pushed my bike through a line of trees and then through the fence into the Soviet War Memorial arena. Leaving my bike on the cobbled drive I walked up to the hunched figure of Mother Homeland, surrounded by weeping birches. Circling the statue I made sure I had the place to myself—I'd seen no signs of a tail this morning, but yesterday's meeting with Dmitri had made me careful. That's one reason I'd cycled here this morning: not only was it the quickest way to get here, but it's hard to follow someone on a bike—too fast to shadow on foot, too slow to track in a vehicle.

But I was all alone, there weren't even any workers setting up for tomorrow's rally, just an army field kitchen trailer abandoned by the entrance arch.

Before me hung the dipped flags of red granite. As I walked up the slope, the figure of the Red Army soldier rose out of the close horizon, stark against the leached sky, sword in one hand, child on the other arm, swastika trampled underfoot. However much things had changed in our land, this place continued to have a strong hold on the nation's collective imagination; the arena was built with a language of power and subjugation. And that was precisely why

Kaminsky had chosen the Soviet War Memorial for his final rally.

Standing between the granite flags, above the field of white sarcophagi and the bronze soldier, I tried to imagine how it would be the next day, thousands of Kaminsky supporters filling the arena. If I were here, amongst his followers, how would I take out Kaminsky? What would be the best angle of attack? On the day itself he would be standing on the barrow at the far end, before the plinth on which the twelve metre high bronze soldier stood. Kaminsky would be looking straight at where I was standing now. He'd be high above the masses, anyone trying to get to him would first have to climb the steps, dodging police and Party toughs.

There would only be one way to kill Kaminsky—to use a gun.

From the edge of the site I could see through the fence to the park beyond. There were very few places with an unobstructed line of sight towards the plinth. Post a police officer at each of those points and there could be no danger from that angle.

That meant, to get a clear shot, the assassin would have to come into the arena itself. Anyone in this area could shoot Kaminsky.

But would they get away afterwards?

I climbed the barrow to the Red Soldier's plinth. Built into the stonework was a crypt, a mosaic lined sanctuary. There was nowhere there to hide, but what about explosives? Instinctively I shrugged away the idea—too unfocussed: there would be no way to guarantee Kaminsky's death. I wandered around the outside of the plinth, looking closely at the joints in the stonework. The stained limestone showed no signs of tampering, no fresh scratches or crumbling edges. Turning around, looking out over the arena before me I thought of the hundreds of places where explosives could be hidden.

The cenotaphs were hollow, or what about under the lawns? But these options were no good if Kaminsky were the target, they could only harm the crowd.

Perhaps that was the aim? A terrorist attack on a large gathering of people, designed to cause indiscriminate injury, the senselessness creating widespread fear.

The GDR had been lucky, we'd never yet been the target of a terrorist operation. But in places where attacks had happened there had always been a tightening of the reins, a new package of 'law and order' measures, tying the population down, winding back the clock on civil liberties and human rights. That would suit Kaminsky just fine, it would strengthen his arguments for strong leadership. A scapegoat would be found—a refugee, or maybe some well-known political figure, one who was progressive, one who opposed Kaminsky and his policies.

My musings raised a new question: what if Kaminsky, far from being the intended target, what if he were the intended beneficiary of the attack?

Speculation. Absurd speculation. Even my cynical friend Dmitri hadn't voiced any concerns about the possibility of an attack. Steinlein was the only one who believed in an assassination plot, and his fears were based only on uncorroborated material from an unknown source.

I was finished here. There was nothing to see, nothing to do, no evidence of a conspiracy. I'd given Steinlein the help I'd promised and I'd paid a heavy price for my generosity. I'd tell Steinlein I was quitting, then go home and get some rest.

I was about to set off down the steps when I heard the jangling of a chain and the creak of rusty hinges. The sound came from behind me, from the back of the arena. I moved around the side of the stone plinth, expecting to see a workforce arriving to set up the infrastructure for the rally. Instead, I saw a *Volkspolizei* patrol car, the boot open. Two police officers heaved a wooden box out, and, stumbling under the weight, carried it through the gates.

The cops didn't see me, they were concentrating on the chest they were carefully lowering to the ground. One pulled away a section of the stone panelling below the fence. It moved easily, revealing a void in the stonework. They slotted the box into the space, and levered the stonework back into position.

When the policemen had shut the gates and driven off I went to where they had hidden the box. The low wall was engraved with quotes from Stalin, and in places it was in a poor state, the cement crumbling under the pressure of swelling tree roots. I pulled at the stone flag, feeling it loosen. Another tug, and it came away, crunching onto the gravel at my feet.

And behind it sat an olive-green ammunition box. Pulling the box out a little, I used my penknife to lever the wooden lid off. I pulled the greaseproof paper aside to reveal a clutch of smoke grenades and ten Makarov hand pistols.

The sun was already high, heat stabbing through the foliage overhanging the fence. I checked my watch, it was nearly 12 o'clock, I was supposed to meet Steinlein in half an hour.

As I walked back to my bike I considered what I'd found. I'd put the box back in the hole, I wasn't happy about leaving the arms there, but they were too heavy to carry, and I couldn't see any other solution.

I'd been tempted by the idea that Kaminsky was a terrorist but the arms cache told a different story, one more compatible with Steinlein's theory that Kaminsky was the target. But why would they need so many pistols? And what were the smoke grenades for?

I was back on Stralau within twenty minutes, arriving before Steinlein. While I waited for him I had another look at the blueprint of the Soviet War Memorial. I was marking the site of the cache when I heard my partner's stick tapping up the stairs.

"I bring news!" Steinlein was now in the room. "The chair of the Central Round Table is going to be at the rally tomorrow—she'll be up there with Kaminsky."

Steinlein's information surprised me: time and again Hanna Krause had been publicly humiliated by Kaminsky, what had happened to make her agree to stand alongside him? But I couldn't let myself be sidetracked, I told Steinlein about the cache.

"This is it!" Steinlein was actually excited, it was the closest I'd ever seen him to being happy. "This confirms what I've been saying all along-"

"But why do they need all those guns? What are they planning?"

"A kidnapping," the policeman answered immediately. "It *looks* like a kidnapping, but it can't be."

"But if it is a kidnapping-"

"It isn't. That's against all the evidence—a kidnapping is too messy, too unpredictable. Only an amateur would try to kidnap Kaminsky in the middle of a rally."

"Assassination or kidnapping—it doesn't matter. The two of us won't be able to stop either of those things. It's time to hand it over to the experts, get Unit 9 involved. There's more than enough evidence-"

"No!" Steinlein moved closer, his eyes widening. "We can't trust Unit 9—we have to find another way."

"There is no other way! Be realistic, we have to go to the Ministry and tell them what we've found out. Let them deal with it."

"Are you even listening to what I'm saying?" Steinlein was leaning closer, both hands on his walking stick. "If we go to the Ministry then the other side will get wind of it. We can't take that chance. They'll postpone their plans and next time we may not hear about it in time. Going to the Ministry isn't the way forward, I've got this under control!"

I shook my head, there was no way Steinlein had this under control.

"There are ten pistols in that box." I was trying to be reasonable, put the facts before Steinlein one last time. "And there's smoke grenades. There's going to be at least ten people involved in the kidnapping, or the assassination, or whatever it is. Ten people! There's no way you and I can stop ten of them!"

"It's under control. It's too late to mess with the plan!"

I didn't like what was happening, Steinlein was genuinely angry, even more so than yesterday—his face red, the knuckles over his cane white, his other hand was a fist, held just in front of my chest.

"What plan? What do you mean?" I asked, swallowing down my own temper.

Steinlein hesitated, but his cane carried on shaking. "*Our* plan: we agreed we'd look into this together, that we wouldn't tell anyone-"

"I agreed to help you look into it, and I have. But now I'm saying this is too big for two invalids to handle!"

"I've got this under control—trust me!"

But I didn't trust Steinlein. I agreed with him that the Party and the police were still close—particularly elite squads like Unit 9. But I was beginning to ask myself why Steinlein was so resistant to making our investigation official.

14:12
Martin

The Ministry appeared to be populated entirely by nervous civil servants, all intent on palliating stress by means of dashing around and appearing indispensable. It took me half an hour to parley my way through the over-excited masses and reach a member of the Ministerial Committee. When I finally entered Timo Rosen's office he was arguing with Hanna Krause, the chair of the Central Round Table.

"After all the names he's called you, all the times he-" Timo broke off when he saw me by the door. "What is it?"

I looked uncertainly from Hanna to Rosen. He was standing in the middle of the office, red-faced, while Hanna sat drinking tea in a comfy chair.

"Comrade Minister, my name is Martin Grobe from RS-"

"Martin! Come in, I haven't seen you since ..." Hanna had got out of her chair and was coming to meet me, holding her hands out. "It must have been 1990? Can it really be four years?"

Rosen remained where he was, arms crossed and mouth set as he watched the reunion.

I explained why I'd come, and after listening for a few minutes, Rosen pressed a button on his intercom. "Get the boys from Glinkastrasse over here."

"And if you needed yet another reason not to do this ..." he told Hanna.

"Politics isn't always pure and simple, you know that better than anyone, Timo." Hanna answered. "Lots of people have put their trust in Kaminsky, it's our job to listen to them."

Rosen ignored Hanna's answer, slotting a pair of reading glasses over the bridge of his nose and looking at the leaked reports I'd brought.

"I'll leave you two to it," Hanna said, patting me on the arm. "We should get together soon, bring Laura and Erika. Let's get this horrible rally business out of the way first and then I want to hear your thoughts on how we can get the referendum result on the Round Tables implemented."

Hanna left just as a lieutenant from Unit 9 was announced. He saluted and immediately began sifting through material I'd brought.

"What do you think, comrade Lieutenant Ziegler?" asked Rosen.

"Hard to say, comrade Minister. There's something fishy

here but there's nothing concrete, if you see what I mean."

"And what about the arms cache, is that not concrete enough for you?" Rosen and Ziegler shifted their gaze to me. One shocked, the other dispassionate yet attentive.

"What arms cache would that be, comrade Captain?" asked Ziegler.

I described the box I'd found behind the stone slabs, and the policeman reached for the telephone, swiftly despatching a squad to pick it up.

"Anything else you'd care to share, comrade Captain? Because now would be a really good time."

I spent the afternoon at the table with several Unit 9 officers, answering questions as fully as I could without mentioning Steinlein. The elite police squad sifting through the plans had immediately recognised the significance of the material I'd brought. Ziegler spent much of the time leaning against the wall, listening to what we were discussing. He was behind me but I could feel his eyes on my back, he didn't bother to look away when I turned around, content for me to know that I was under scrutiny.

"Are you telling us everything, comrade Captain?" he asked at one point.

"I don't think I've forgotten anything."

His eyes rested on mine, trying to ferret out whatever secret I was keeping from him.

"Why didn't you come to us earlier?"

"As I said, I wasn't convinced that this was a serious threat."

"Someone passes you the security plans for Dr. Kaminsky's rally and you don't consider it to be serious?"

He was right, he was definitely right. Why hadn't I come sooner? I'd allowed my own doubts to cloud my judgement, allowed Steinlein to lull me into complacency, ignored my instinct and experience.

It was obvious the lieutenant wasn't satisfied, but it wasn't his place to question me. For the time being he could only work with the material I had delivered.

The police unit drew up their plans and got Minister Rosen to sign the paperwork. They would provide a close protection detail for Kaminsky, some wearing standard issue *Volkspolizei* uniforms, others in plain clothes, mixing in with stewards and invited guests.

"Make sure you don't get this wrong. It's bad enough that Kaminsky's at risk, but now the Chair of the Central Round Table has taken it into her head to be there as well ..."

Rosen was fretting.

21:27
Martin

Steinlein waited for me at the top of the stairs, both hands clenching the top of his walking stick.

"Where have you been?"

I moved past him into our office. "At the Ministry, talking to Unit 9."

He stared at me for a few moments, eyes narrowed almost to slits. "Well, we might as well pack up now, that's it—it's all over."

"Unit 9 are going to provide close protection to Kaminsky. They're taking the threat seriously. And Minister Rosen is on the case, he'll be receiving hourly reports and will be in constant contact during the event."

"Dietmar Rosen? Just another hack, covering his own back!"

"Our informant gave us detailed plans. It was my duty to pass on that information."

"Perhaps. Maybe you're right. At least now they can't act surprised when it happens, not now they know RS is involved." Steinlein's voice was muted, but then his head snapped up. "Did you mention me?"

I shook my head and Steinlein relaxed.

"My name didn't come up at all?"

"No. I told them I was acting on my own initiative. They think I was following up a tip-off."

"Good, good." Steinlein seemed to gain energy again. "Good work." He got up from the chair and headed for the stairs. "I better get back to the station, still lots to do, meetings and briefings. I'll meet you in Treptow in the morning. I'll be there from 0600 hours, doing a sweep of the park with my squad."

That went better than expected. I breathed a sigh of relief and was about to sit in the chair just vacated by Steinlein before I realised there wasn't anything else to do. We'd done all we could, and tomorrow we would find out if it had been enough.

"Can you give me a lift?" I shouted down the stairs.

"I can drop you off at Ostkreuz."

21:46
Karo

I needed to be doing something, and tracking down Becker was all I had left. I was so close to him, I could feel it in my belly; I wanted to go somewhere he'd been, get a feel for him. Hippy shit, I know, but that's how I felt.

I cycled down the main road on Stralau. The bottle plant stank, but it was nothing compared to the oily smell coming from the asphalt factory and the pukeworthy maltiness hanging around the feed mill. I wasn't exactly sure where the *Durchgangsheim* was but Erika had told me it was a big red-brick building on the left.

There it was, past the factories. Just two storeys and a lower ground floor, bars on the windows and doors.

Behind me there was banging and smells of burnt metal coming from a boatyard, but the red brick building before me was dead. A kind of shadow hung over it, even though the sun was still high, shining directly on it, lighting up every cracked brick, every line of soot and every splash of dirt on the windows. All the curtains were drawn so I couldn't see in. I rattled the main door then walked to the side but there was a high wall topped with broken glass blocking my way. I went back to the front and tried to peer through the thin curtains. All I could see were dusty cobwebs.

I could break in, there was nobody around, and more than enough noise was coming from the boatyard to cover the sound of breaking glass.

Except I'd just be chasing ghosts.

That was when I saw the Lada, it went straight past me and I could see Martin in the passenger seat. I was about to wave when I saw the person driving. Something about him made me stop. I don't know why, I didn't recognise him—or I did, but I couldn't place him. He looked familiar, but not in a good way.

As the car disappeared around the curve I just stood there, wondering what Martin was doing here, and why the person driving the Lada was giving me the heebie-jeebies.

DAY 7
Saturday
18th June 1994

Today I come to Berlin. Today I will stand at the Soviet War Memorial, that monument to the sacrifices of our Soviet brothers in the Great Patriotic War against Fascism. Because today we are in the middle of a new struggle, a struggle against the anti-democratic forces ranged against us: the saboteurs, the nay-sayers, the anti-social elements.

Today I meet the people of the Capital of the GDR, and I will listen, just as I have listened to all the people who came to see me in each and every city and town of this Republic.

Some say that my journey around our country has been the tour of a narcissist. But all who come to my gatherings know to expect such egregious lies from the elite. The people who come to my gatherings know that it's not about me, it's about them. They have chosen me, and I have listened to their worries and their concerns.

Today my journey ends. After this interview, I will leave this studio and I will go and speak to the biggest assembly of all. People from all over the Republic, right now, are making their way to Berlin to be with me.

Because today I will listen once again. And then I will go back to the seat of government, and I will act.

Martin

Kaminsky made his way through the crowd, flanked by flunkies and stewards. Others went before their leader, holding the old GDR flag and forging a path through the sweating sea of fanatics. The chants were all around them: *Kaminsky Kaminsky Kaminsky.*

I was near the back, on the west side, but I could see Kaminsky clearly enough: crisp, unbothered by the limp humidity trapped in the arena. Along with thousands of others I watched him leave the sump of supporters, climbing up the steps of the barrow. He moved purposefully towards the open gate of the crypt in the pedestal of the bronze soldier. In his arms he held a large wreath, a black, red and yellow ribbon plaited between the foliage. He placed it just inside the chamber. The stewards hushed the crowd, and for a moment, while Kaminsky bowed his head, a whole *Volk* was silent.

Kaminsky slowly turned around. He surveyed the still masses assembled in the heat below, then he raised a fist, unleashing a clamour that rolled through the arena, rumbling forward until it washed against the low hill.

Kaminsky Kaminsky Kaminsky!

A warm breeze drifted up the river, setting trees rustling, cheering Kaminsky on.

But Kaminsky stood, his fist still in the air.

Kaminsky waited as the chants tumbled over his supporters.

Starting from the front, edging back through the crowd, an expectant silence fell. Kaminsky stepped up to the microphones. The wind had brought up steel clouds, roiling through the sky and pooling Kaminsky in a grey light. He was savouring the moment, the power he had to command his legions of followers.

"Today," his voice warm, intimate, letting the microphones

do their work. "Today is *our* day!"

Again the crowd erupted, and Kaminsky stepped back, allowing the people to shout their approval.

"Today is our day. We've come a long way, we've taken a hard road together, and here we are—the people!" Another lull, the sound of the cheers still lapping the arena.

"But this is not the end of our road. This is only the beginning! *We haven't even started!*"

The radio unit slung from my shoulder crackled in the charged air. I raised the tiny speaker to my ear. *All units report.* I kept tally as each unit gave their status, starting from the centre and radiating out until Steinlein announced: *Berta 7, keine besonderen Vorkommnisse.* So far, so good.

Kaminsky was still speaking, the people around me intent, focussed on this one man. He was projecting his voice now, the loudspeakers struggling against the agitation of the trees. The breeze was freshening, loosening the close air, a storm was coming.

"No longer will we be treated as second class citizens!

"No longer will we let the politicians and the bureaucrats do as they please! We, the people, are on the march! We the people are dealing with the problems the elite don't care about. It's time for common sense. *Our* common sense will prevail!"

Kaminsky held out his arms, his hands pushing back the adulation of his followers. *Kaminsky Kaminsky!* Beneath the trembling throb of a hundred thousand voices I could feel the susurrance of the approaching storm.

"And common sense is breaking out—we are already winning! Beside me today is someone we all know. Yes, it's someone with whom we've had our disagreements, and that makes it all the more significant that she's chosen to be with us.

"My friends, citizens of the GDR, I give you the chair of the Central Round Table, Hanna Krause!" The rustle of the trees became a roar, perfectly matching the pitch of Kaminsky's voice.

And that was when the lightning struck. It came before the rain, a clean spike of light, slicing the air, striking the bronze soldier—the smell of carbon and ozone cauterising the festivities. Kaminsky and the other speakers on the plinth fell, separating like twigs and leaves shaken from the trees around us. Even at this distance, even in the iron light of the clouds I see the mouths opening to scream. But one figure didn't scream, one figure didn't stand to flee down the steps. Only one figure remained lying at the feet of the Soviet soldier.

The heavy rain fell as waves of thunder crashed in.

PART 2
Guerilla Politics

DAY 7
Saturday
18th June 1994

Berlin: *There have been reports of casualties after a terrorist attack at a rally in Treptower Park. Early indications are of at least one death after shots were fired at an event called by the General Secretary of the PDS, Dr. Kaminsky. Further injuries were sustained during the evacuation of the site. Ambulances are attending the scene.*

13:17
Martin

A hand was on my arm, pulling me. Steinlein.

A last look towards the *Bonzen* coming down from the plinth—Unit 9 officers had surrounded Kaminsky and were shuffling him away, other officers knelt by the fallen body. The radio set was squawking, static from the storm threatening to submerge the words: *Ambulance required, repeat ambulance required.*

Steinlein had hold of me, he was thrusting his way through the panic, his uniform making people give way even as they struggled to escape. Under the triumphal arch, onto the road. The rain was falling heavily now—bloated drops that stuck to the cobblestones, filling the gutters and flowing over the curb. A uniformed policeman opened the door of a black Volga, an absurd, drenched salute as I was pushed in. Steinlein took the wheel, blue lights scratching the soused air. He pulled into the road, sluicing through the escaping masses, away from the rally and the body of my old friend Hanna Krause.

DAY 8
Sunday
19th June 1994

Berlin: *The death of Hanna Krause has been confirmed. Frau Krause, chair of the Central Round Table of the GDR, died in the Charité Clinic early this morning after being wounded at Dr. Kaminsky's rally yesterday. Police are pursuing several lines of enquiry, but are currently focussing on the possibility that Dr. Kaminsky himself was the intended target.*

04:41
Martin

From my chair I watched the morning sky lift from flat grey to washed-out blue. There was no music playing, the turntable stood still, the pickup arm rested on its cradle. A cigarette smouldered between my fingers, a couple of bottles of schnapps lay empty on the floor beside me.

Hanna Krause was dead.

Kaminsky should have taken the bullet.

I hadn't stopped it from happening, I had to live with that.

Hanna had been one of us, one of the opposition. She'd been with us in the old days, putting her life and her family on the line, fighting injustice, desperate for change.

There were no tears in me. There was no sadness. Only rage. Furious, impotent rage.

From the rally, Steinlein and I had headed straight to our little office on Stralau. We'd cleaned the place thoroughly, taken away every scrap of paper, every pen and pencil. We'd wiped down every surface, removed every fingerprint and trace of occupancy. When we were done there was nothing left to mark our investigation, not even footprints in the dust.

I came home and drank a bottle of schnapps. I sat through the night, hating myself for not preventing Hanna's death.

11:56
Martin

They came for me at midday. There was no knock, just a kick to the door. Steinlein brought them, Steinlein took me away.

13:55
Martin

"Let's take it from the top, we need to get our story straight."

Steinlein was sweating, he'd put his uniform cap on the table and undone the top few buttons of his blouson. Now he was holding a pen, ready to write down whatever I said.

We were in an interview room, both of us sitting at the table. I was still drunk, still trying to understand what had happened. Hanna Krause had been shot. Despite Unit 9, despite all the material we'd uncovered. Despite everything.

I sat up straight, trying to sober up, to order my thoughts. But the memory of the lightning flash, her figure falling, the realisation that she would never get up again ... How long had I known Hanna? Ten years? Now she was gone. Why her? Why not Kaminsky? Why always the good people?

Steinlein was right, we needed to get our story straight. The twin reel tape recorder on the table was still, this was between me and Steinlein's pen.

"Everything?" I asked, still trying to stop my brain from replaying those moments at the Soviet War Memorial. I waited for Steinlein to nod. Everything.

"I'm on leave from the *Republikschutz*, and you approached me—when was it? Just over a week ago." I was trying to breathe properly. Steady, regular breaths. I watched the lieutenant's face closely, searching for a clue as to what to include, what to leave out.

But Steinlein hadn't reacted, his pen hadn't touched paper.

"I received an anonymous tip-off a week ago," I tried again. Steinlein's pen started scratching at the rough greyness of the form, taking down what I was saying.

I gave him an account, edited him out, took responsibility for everything we'd done together. At the end I was shivering, I was thinking about Krause, about Kaminsky's lucky escape, about the whole bloody mess. About our failure.

Steinlein left the room, closing the door behind him. I sat in the chair, indifferent to my fate.

It was another ten minutes before the lock clicked open.

"Comrade Captain, would you accompany us?" a constable requested, politely enough, but with that hint of steel that police officers must practice.

He led the way, a police recruit taking up the rear of our convoy as we went along corridors and down stairs to the custody area. A sergeant stood behind the desk, ready to receive his new guest.

"Martin Grobe, presented for detention," the constable announced.

At a signal from the sergeant the constable pulled my left arm behind my back. I bent over in pain, my head hitting the desk. The recruit emptied my pockets and the sergeant documented my belongings.

"Reason for detention?"

"Criminal Code paragraphs 112 and 99."

The desk sergeant wrote down the paragraph numbers, murmuring to himself as he did so: "Murder. Terrorism."

DAY 9
Monday
20th June 1994

Aktuelle Kamera: Tell me about your bill to disband the Round Tables—does the timing have anything to do with what happened at the weekend?

Kaminsky: The appalling murder of Hanna Krause was an attack on us all. The tragic events of Saturday have changed politics in this country forever. It was a terrorist attack, and this country will never give in to terror. Nevertheless, we need to respond, and to respond quickly. I am calling for a full investigation into what happened. Those responsible will be made to pay for their mistakes.

But let's be clear about this, the outrage happened because this incompetent government allowed it to. We have a weak government and the source of that weakness is the Round Tables.

The Round Tables have no legal status, yet these unelected groups are telling our government what it should do.

Aktuelle Kamera: You say the Round Tables have no legal standing, but in April the country voted in a referendum to change the constitution in order to give the Round Tables and the Workers' Councils more power.

Kaminsky: Yes, they did. And this is an excellent example of political manipulation. That referendum should have never been held. Why? To answer that we need to look at who called for the referendum, and who came up with the questions. It was the

Round Tables themselves! Nowhere in our constitution does it say that the Round Tables can call referenda. The democratically elected representatives of the people, sitting in the Volkskammer, opposed this referendum. They had good reason to, and they explained their reasons very clearly in parliament—it wasn't just my party—the CDU and the SPD also opposed the referendum. All the major parties opposed the referendum, but they were outmanoeuvred by the self-selected and self-serving Round Tables —a group of people more interested in their own public profile than in the democracy we fought so long and hard for. These conditions lead to anarchy and to the violence we saw on Saturday.

Aktuelle Kamera: *Do you and your party accept the result of the referendum?*

Kaminsky: *A small group of individuals are seeking personal power—individuals who are neither able nor willing to put themselves forward as candidates in a democratic election. There isn't another country in the world that would put up with such shenanigans. Groups of people are gathering together in living rooms and village halls with the sole aim of putting pressure on our democratic institutions. The so-called Central Round Table presumes to interfere in government business. Our democratically elected government is at the beck and call of a shadowy, unaccountable cabal.*

That isn't democracy, it's guerilla politics.

Aktuelle Kamera: *The Round Tables say they are open to all, are transparent and accountable. They talk about safeguards such as shadowing, regular rotation and powers of immediate recall by any of the lower levels. Do you accept that this is just a different way of doing democracy?*

Kaminsky: *I was elected by the people, and my job as a member of the Volkskammer is to uphold the constitution, to guard it to the best of my abilities. And while I remain a democratically elected member of parliament, I shall continue to do just that.*

Karo

Erika had domesticated me. Here I was, we'd only just had breakfast and I was doing the dishes before we went to work. Obviously not the way I'd choose to spend my mornings, but Erika was putting me up so I had to show willing.

"What do you want on your sandwiches?" she asked.

"Don't care."

There was a silence for a bit, just the clattering of dishes and the news on the radio spreading fear and unease. We were both still shocked by Hanna's death. It felt like something had ended and something much worse was about to begin. It felt like the whole country was holding its breath, wondering what would come next.

Kaminsky knew this. He was whipping up the fear levels, talking about the state's failure, the need for strong measures against saboteurs and terrorists.

I rinsed the glasses.

"Erika—were you ever followed, in the old days, I mean?"

"We all were. Surely everyone who was politically active was followed. Weren't you?"

I thought about it. Looking back it was clear that I had been, but usually just a police car or uniformed officers, trying to make me feel uncomfortable. This was different.

"It's just, I've been having this strange feeling, you know, like I'm not alone. Probably just being paranoid."

Erika went over to the radio and turned the volume up. Right up.

"Why did you do that?" I asked.

Erika stared at the radio in surprise. "Oh, habit I suppose. Tell me more about this feeling."

"It's probably nothing. Just on edge after Saturday."

"How long have you had this feeling?" Erika wasn't letting this one go, even though I was now totally sure I was just being paranoid. Talking about it was making me feel stupid.

"Since Friday afternoon."

"Since you asked Captain Neumann about Becker?"

Put it that way and it sounded less stupid. Still paranoid though. "But that sort of thing doesn't happen any more-"

"It happened to Martin last autumn."

"Yeah, but that was when he was chasing some Stasi dudes who still hadn't got the fact that the old days are over."

"I'm not so certain the old days are over," replied Erika.

We had a plan. Like all the best plans, Erika said, it's simple. I was to leave for work first, and Erika was to watch at the window. She even had this home-made periscope thing so she wouldn't be seen.

"How long have you had that?" There was me thinking I was paranoid but having a periscope was on a whole other level.

"Years. Made it with my daughter when she was little." She examined the periscope, the dark cardboard had scribbles of coloured pencil all over it.

"You have a daughter?" Shit, I didn't even know this basic fact about Erika's life!

"Jenni. I don't see her so often any more, she's studying engineering in Ilmenau." Erika was fiddling with the periscope. "Shall we see if this trick still works?"

I left the building, didn't look around but went straight to the bakery (my turn to get the bread rolls for the office second breakfast). The whole time I was trying to be dead nonchalant, deliberately not keeping an eye out for anybody I might have seen once too often, not listening out for the scrape of a shoe on concrete, just making my merry whistling way to the bakery, then on to work.

Erika was already at the office by the time I got there, she must have overtaken me while I was buying the bread.

"Well?"

"You're right. You're being followed."

"This isn't happening, it can't be true! Why would they want to follow me? Who would want to follow me?"

"I didn't get a good look, but she looked familiar, like I knew her, but didn't. It'll come to me." Erika bustled around, unpacking the rolls, putting them on a plate. "I think we should assume this is to do with Becker. Tell me again, what happened when you saw Captain Neumann on Friday."

"He said they were too busy, come back on Monday—which is today."

"Nothing else? Did he say why they were too busy?"

"Because of the rally. So I asked him what he had to do with that because it's in a completely different district, and he said that Treptow had asked for administrative assistance because there was some kind of threat to Kaminsky."

"A threat?"

I shrugged my shoulders. What did she expect? Did she think I'd just walk into the cop shop and start interrogating the hardest hard-ass bull I could find?

"Have you checked the Stasi archive for any mentions of Becker?"

"He's clean. I couldn't even find any reports *about* him, never mind *by* him."

"Nothing? Nothing at all? How thorough were you?"

I was getting a bit antsy now. It was like Erika was checking I was doing my job properly. Not that it was my job. Nor any of her business either.

"I just did the usual F16 search, the person index."

"So you didn't check for reports about him?"

"Erika, will you back off! I did the checks, alright?"

"Karo, calm down. You're being followed, and we're trying to work out who by. Being defensive isn't helping."

"I'm not being defensive!"

"So did you check anything beyond the F16 cards?"

I shook my head, and Erika finally backed off. I watched her sit down and stare out of the window. Her eyes were blank, she was thinking.

"What other names did you give Neumann?" Erika was back with us.

I pulled out the sheet of paper, it was still in my pocket, and I smoothed it out a bit before handing it over.

"Let's take this to the morning meeting," she said.

"What exactly did Neumann say about threats to Kaminsky?" Klaus had the same question as Erika.

"He just said that Lichtenberg police were helping Treptow out with some threat." They were all being super-serious about the fact that I may or may not have a stalker. It was dead embarrassing and made me feel patronised.

"Look, I can take care of myself, there's no need to be so worried about it."

"Last year, Martin told us he was being followed and we didn't take him seriously. That was a mistake," Erika replied. Laura and Klaus nodded, both looking anywhere but at Erika and me.

Klaus moved the subject back a step, maybe he'd noticed I was feeling uncomfortable, but he was probably still focussed on the information I had about the rally.

"I don't like what Neumann said. We haven't been told anything about this threat, but we should have been—that's what RS is there for."

"We are being wound up, a few more weeks and there won't be any RS any more."

"Still, a matter of courtesy, if nothing else. And anyway there may be some kind of link between Karo being tailed and what happened on Saturday." Klaus wasn't letting this go.

"I'm going to see Antje at the Ministry later, I'll talk to her about it," Erika offered.

Klaus nodded, stroking his lame moustache.

★

133

The deal was that I wasn't to go *anywhere* alone. I was *always* to be accompanied by a responsible adult, aka my RS colleagues.

So that meant I got to come to the Ministry with Erika, and in return she got to join me on my visit to Neumann. It all felt way over the top, but I kind of liked the idea of not having to face Neumann alone. He gave me the creeps.

"We need to work out what the threat level is. Why are they following you? Is it to find out what you're up to, to intimidate you, or something worse?"

I didn't like the sound of the something-worse option but didn't really want to think about it either.

"Why can't I just go to the cops, tell them I've got a stalker?" I didn't want to ask the cops for help with anything, but that's what they're there for, and if they can't even deal with something like this ...

"Seriously, Karo? Right now the cops are going to be running around in circles trying to work out what to do about last Saturday. And anyway, we're wondering whether Neumann *ordered* the tail, so I'd say that rules out going to the police."

Great, that made me feel really stupid. Thanks, Erika. Still, it was interesting that Erika and the others seemed to trust the bulls even less than I did. I hadn't realised they were that critical, particularly since they work with the cops so much. But here was Erika making me feel bourgeois and naïve.

"So who's Antje?" I asked.

"She's one of the three members on the Ministerial Committee. She and I are old friends—we used to do stuff together in our Women's group, back in 1988 and 1989. She went into politics at the start of the revolution, joined *Neues Forum* just before I got roped into RS."

But Antje didn't seem very friendly when we got to the Ministry. We were kept waiting in some meeting room by a hardcore secretary, and then when Antje came in she looked really stressed.

"Erika, didn't my secretary phone to cancel? I don't have time-"

But Erika just stood up and pulled a chair out. "Antje, sit down. Karo, go and sort out some coffee." Erika was dead confident, I hadn't seen her like this before.

I hung around in the doorway for a moment, looking at Antje, a tall woman with a really cool hairstyle (she had it done up in this ironic grey bun at the back of her head). She sat down and let out a weird, squeaky gasp. "I'm sorry Erika, it's all gone crazy. Kaminsky has called a special session in the *Volkskammer*, I've been summoned ..."

I went out to the nasty secretary and told her to bring three coffees, and pastries too. The secretary gave me a stern look, as if she'd caught me lying, but she pressed a button on her oversized telephone and passed on the request.

When I went back into the room Antje was still talking, but she broke off when she saw me.

"It's OK, this is Karo. She's our newest recruit. You can trust her."

Antje held out her hand and gave me a polite smile, but immediately turned back to Erika.

"Kaminsky has tabled a motion to suspend the Round Tables. He says the referendum result can't be allowed to stand, not after this act of terrorism. He's already got a law and order bill prepared, and he's demanding the Round Tables be completely closed down."

"He can't do that! The people won't let him!" I blurted out, then turned bright red.

"I'm sorry, Karo is it? I think he may manage to do exactly that. The legislation mandated by the referendum hasn't been enacted yet, the *Volkskammer* can simply refuse to vote it through. And as for the people," Antje breathed out heavily, "until a few weeks ago, I might have agreed with you. But it's like the word *Volk* has changed its meaning. Just a short while ago it meant everyone in the country, but now it seems much of the population supports Kaminsky and his new definitions."

The secretary came in with a tray which she slid onto the table. Cups and a coffee pot, but no pastries.

"I told you to bring cake!" I hissed at her, but she ignored me.

"Was there any prior intelligence on the attack at the rally?" asked Erika.

Antje looked up in surprise. "Your colleague, Martin Grobe, he turned up on Friday with a sackful of material."

"Martin?"

OK, that was weird. One: Martin was meant to be on leave. Two: if Martin had found anything suspicious then he would have talked to us. And three: well, I couldn't think of a number three, but that didn't make it any the less disturbing.

"Martin didn't mention any of this," I told Antje, but she just shrugged, she didn't seem interested. "We want to be involved. In the investigation, I mean."

"In an oversight capacity," added Erika. "We thought it wise, considering the Party connections."

Antje thought for a moment, then went over to a telephone in the corner of the room. "I'll check in with Timo and Mario."

While Antje was talking to the other members of the Ministerial Committee, Erika squidged her face up at me. "Why do we want to be involved?" she whispered.

"Because it's our job! I bet Klaus really wants to do it, and I thought we could maybe, I don't know, *do* something."

"Do something? Do what exactly?"

Erika really wasn't getting this, but I couldn't find the words to explain myself. We had to stop Kaminsky, and maybe this would give us a way to do that. Although, thinking about it more, it probably wouldn't help and would just create more work. OK, maybe it was a shit idea, but it was too late now. Still, nice of Erika to back me up.

"Timo and Mario are fine with you participating—in principle. We'll have to be careful about the parameters of your activities, particularly considering Kaminsky's dislike of your department. In the meantime I've asked the Police Minister to send someone up to brief you."

Antje stood by her chair while she finished off her coffee.

"Right, back to the grindstone. I'll make-"

The door burst open, and a man crashed in. It was one of those grey men that seem to breed in government offices, except he was more red than grey. His face was flushed and he was panting as if he'd just run up all the stairs in the whole ministry.

"Frau *Ministerin* Willehardt, there's a problem." But he stopped when he saw me and Erika.

"What is it Herr Winkler? Don't worry, these are colleagues from RS."

But Winkler just went even redder. I was starting to enjoy my trip to the Ministry.

"Come, on, spit it out!" Antje wasn't a patient woman. She turned to us and said: "Herr Winkler is the Police Minister."

Winkler spluttered a bit more, then spat it out. "RS can't possibly be involved in any investigation."

Antje fixed him with this awesome glare that would make even Laura look cuddly. The Police Minister didn't stand a chance.

"The suspect," he stammered. "The person being held for the attempted assassination, it's an RS officer called Martin Grobe."

Karo

Erika and I legged it all the way to the station, and then spent the whole journey wishing we could be there already. The Police Minister had said that Martin was up before the judge this morning, it wasn't the proper court case, just a remand hearing. But the first rule of prisoner support is to make sure the prisoner knows they're not alone.

We reckoned that because we were colleagues of Martin there'd be no way they'd let us into the courtroom, so we came up with a plan. I thought it was good enough, Erika was a bit worried it might backfire, but I calmed her down. I'd make it work.

When we got off the train I headed into the little supermarket that used to be just for the Stasi and got myself a couple of small bottles of beer. I took the cap off one, then ran after Erika. I caught up with her just as she was going through the door of the court house, shoving past her and disappearing down a corridor. It didn't take long for a court officer to try to head me off. I pretended to be pissed, not walking straight, and then: trip and pour beer all over the officer's shirt, dodge him as he swears and makes a grab for me. Behind me I could hear Erika tut-tutting loudly and ordering the other court officers to call the police. That was enough, I was out of there. But before I went I smashed the second bottle of beer against the wall.

I got through the doors and shot off down the road, the officer puffing and panting, but left way behind. A look over my shoulder, and I could see Erika at the doors, gesticulating and ordering another load of court officers around. They all gathered at the entrance, keeping an eye on me, and Erika wasn't challenged as she slipped away up the stairs. Result.

After all that excitement I went back to the office and waited for Erika on the street outside. I didn't have to wait long, maybe twenty minutes or so, just enough time to regret having chucked that second bottle of beer instead of bringing it back to drink.

"Did you talk to Martin?" I asked when she turned up.

Erika shook her head. "No, but he saw me, he knows we're looking out for him. Come on, we should let the others know what's going on."

As soon as we were in the office, Erika rounded everyone up and told them what was going on.

"He's being accused of murder, terrorism and committing crimes while in state service. Considering the severity of the accusations the judge has agreed to remand him."

There was silence around the table, everyone was completely gobsmacked. It wasn't like anyone believed Martin would do anything like that, no, the question was how had Martin got caught up in all this. Even by his standards this was a real mess.

"We need a plan of action." Laura had already shifted into getting-things-done mode. "We have to get Martin out of prison, the longer they hold him, the more watertight they'll be able to make their case. Only by getting him out can we help Martin prove he's been framed. First thing to do is to find out what evidence they have against him-"

"The evidence they've *made up*, don't you mean?" I interrupted, but Laura ignored me.

"Then we can work out how to get the charges against him dropped. While that's happening we should make a timeline of what Martin's been doing the last few weeks. We need to do that now, before his trail goes cold—hopefully we can turn up some useful alibis. Once we know exactly what's happening we can start a publicity campaign. That's enough for the next twenty-four hours. Let's meet tomorrow morning to do some proper planning once we know more. Everyone agreed?"

We all nodded, Laura was spot on, as usual.

"I suggest that Erika and I start talking to the Ministry of the Interior and the Ministry of Justice, try to squeeze some information out of them and make arrangements to meet Martin. Klaus and Karo, why don't you start plotting Martin's movements?"

I was impressed by the way my RS colleagues had swung into action. I'd expected them to have a big discussion and to argue about whether or not they were allowed to do this kind of thing. But as it was, within a few minutes we had a plan, and a pile of work to go with it. Klaus and I had a quick confab and he headed off to talk to Martin's neighbours, local shops, that kind of thing. I was to contact Dmitri, and somehow I'd agreed to talk to Katrin. OK, somebody had to talk to her, I was the obvious person, and it would have sounded really crap if I'd refused to go and see her about her dad being arrested. So I agreed and regretted it even before the words were out of my mouth.

15:25
Karo

The conscript in front of the metal gate stopped pacing and stood in my way, feet wide apart, hands on his hips. He was about the same age as me, maybe even younger, but he had a uniform on and a gun slung over his shoulder so he thought he was well hard.

"*Stoi!*"

I never paid much attention in Russian classes at school, but everyone knew that *stoi* meant stop. And it wasn't like I could do anything but *stoi* anyway, there was a locked gate in front of me, for fuck's sake.

"I've got an appointment, can you open up?"

Now I was standing there with my legs wide and hands on hips too (bloody testosterone, it's like it's infectious). I was in a rush and not in a mood to be held up by a kid with a gun.

The Russian guard just shook his head and gave me a load of verbal Cyrillic.

"I have an appointment, let me in," I said really slowly, trying not to get angry. I waved my hands at the gate and the building behind it.

The guard said another bunch of stuff and waved his hands in my face, trying to get me to move back.

"Captain Dmitri," I tried.

I wasn't sure that Dmitri was a captain, and I didn't know his surname, but thought it was worth a try. I hadn't expected this kind of difficulty, after all, getting the appointment had been easy—I'd just phoned the number in Martin's contacts book from his desk drawer. The secretary had been really friendly once I'd said I was from RS, and when I said it was urgent he'd assured me I could come round whenever I wanted.

But now it looked like they weren't going to let me in.

"Dmitri, KGB." I was about to lose my rag, almost shouting at the kid in the uniform. I tried to think of my Russian lessons at school, but all I could come up with was the alphabet. "Kah-djay-bay." At least, that sounded right. Ish. "Dmitri, Captain!"

I could tell the guard was getting even more frustrated than I was, I was worried he was going to get physical on me, but suddenly he stood to attention as the gate clanged open behind him.

Some other soldier, probably an officer, came through the partly opened gate. He ignored the guard, who was still standing, chest out, head back, looking like a dummy in a shop window.

The officer guy didn't say anything, just held his hand out as if he wanted me to give him something. I wasn't sure whether it was a bribe he was after, but if it was then he'd have to make do with my RS pass.

"Who?" he asked, in German.

"Captain Dmitri, kah-djay-bay."

The officer nodded and walked off, back through the gate,

still holding my RS papers. I followed him and nobody stopped me so I reckoned I was getting somewhere.

I didn't get very far, though. The officer stopped at the guard hut, a little box made of corrugated metal, and spoke to the soldier inside. A phone call was made, more rapid Russian that made no sense to me, and the officer handed me my pass back, indicating with a curled forefinger that I should follow him.

Martin had told me good things about Dmitri—he clearly admired the Russian. But when I finally met him (which was after what felt like days of winding through a maze of corridors and rooms) I got a completely different impression. This bloke obviously took great care over his appearance. His uniform would have made my mother happy. It was spotless, pressed, and he was still wearing his tunic even though it was well over 30 degrees outside. But it wasn't his dapper appearance that made me dislike him, it was his show-off eyepatch. It said *look at me, hero of the KGB.* And once he'd opened his gob it didn't get any better, it just confirmed my initial impressions.

"Ah! You are the famous Karo! Our mutual friend Martin has told me much about you. You are most welcome, and I am glad we meet at last."

He just really wound me up, the language sounding warm, but actually it was all about himself, the accent so clipped and exact, yeuch!

"But how is dear Martin? I hear he is still on leave. I wish to go and see him, but ..." he waved his arms around, taking in his office, and the whole building, the whole Russian quarter, as if to say he was so *frightfully* busy that he couldn't *possibly* find the time to go and see his *best* pal.

"Yeah, well, maybe you should have gone to see him while you had the chance."

Dmitri leaned back in his chair, one hand holding the other in front of his belly. He was doing the same eyebrow trick as Neumann.

"Oh, for God's sake! Martin has been arrested. They think he was involved in that thing on Saturday."

Now I had Dmitri's attention, there was a definite eyebrow flicker.

"Can you help him?" I asked.

"As an officer of the Russian forces in Germany I regret I'm not in a position to offer assistance. It is not our place to interfere in the internal affairs of our host country-"

"Firstly," I held up a finger, "you are not an officer of the Russian forces—or do you think I don't know what those blue flashes on your uniform mean?" I held up another finger. "Secondly. I'm not asking you to interfere, just tell us if you know what Martin was up to these last few weeks."

"Thirdly ..." And I ran out of steam. I was going to have to stop doing this first-second-third thing, but then I thought of something. "Thirdly, Martin considers you to be a friend. So maybe you better return the fucking compliment and see if you can't see your way to helping him out!"

"I see you know our friend Martin well." Dmitri gave me a crocodile smile. He got up and moved over to a filing cabinet, taking out a bottle of vodka and a couple of glasses. "Why don't you take a seat? You'll forgive my caution, it is become a second nature over the years. But, please, please sit down. Let us drink a toast—it's customary to seal a new friendship-"

"I don't want fucking vodka." I really did want vodka, a whole bottle would do nicely, but I wasn't going to give him the satisfaction.

Dmitri paused, then let the bottle and glasses disappear back into the filing cabinet. He came back to the desk and sat down opposite me. "Now Martin. Yes, he came to see me ..." Dmitri ruffled a few pages in his desk diary, but I was dead sure that he didn't really need to check. "On Thursday. He said he was trying to stop Kaminsky from being assassinated-"

"Kaminsky?"

"He said he was working with the policeman Steinlein."

Steinlein. Now I heard the name I knew him. He was the person I saw in the car with Martin last Friday—it was like I could see his smug face right now. He'd been in the papers, the fash had beaten him up, and he and Martin were in the magazines. Headlines: *Heroes of the Resurgence.*

"And why was Martin working with Steinlein?"

Dmitri angled forward across his desk, and in a voice so low I had to lean over to catch what he said: "I asked him that exact question. And his reply? Steinlein wanted their little project to remain secret, not even the colleagues in RS should know."

"So Steinlein knows what Martin was up to?"

"More than that, the whole project started with Steinlein."

"Steinlein was in on it? Has he been arrested too? Kaminsky is going to crucify them!"

"No, no. I don't think that is likely. Kaminsky is clever, he knows he has had his impact."

"You mean Kaminsky planned this whole thing—that it was staged?"

"I don't know, but I certainly believe it was more than staged, young lady. After all, they shot someone. But perhaps our first concern should be how to get Martin off the hook."

I got out of my chair and headed for the door. I'd heard enough; it wasn't the *young lady* bit, it was Dmitri himself. I knew his type, sit there and talk while others do the work. I had the information I needed.

"Are you always this *grosskotzig*?" I asked when I got to the door.

"*Grosskotzig*?" Dmitri looked puzzled, it probably wasn't very often he came across an unfamiliar German word.

I had to think for a moment before I could come up with an explanation he'd understand. "Pretentious and arrogant."

Dmitri laughed. The whole thing was just a joke to him.

Martin

I heard the key scrape in the lock and got up to stand at the back of my cell, already well schooled in the protocol of prison. But when the door opened it wasn't a grey uniformed warder who came in—it was Karl Kaminsky.

He looked less imposing up close, smaller than on the television or at his rallies. Despite the Western suit and sleek hair he looked like a real person.

I stayed at the back of the cell. I had no desire to take his hand, to greet him. Nor did I want to sit down on the stool again—I preferred to remain standing, to meet Kaminsky at eye-level.

Kaminsky gave my cell the once-over, then allowed his gaze to settle back on me.

"So, this is the man who wanted to kill me. I'm surprised you had it in you. So close, and yet so far away." His hand fluttered in the air, Hanna's soul leaving her body.

"Do you believe in anything?" I don't know where that came from—all the things I could say to him yet my mouth opens and a question like that spills out.

"Believe? What do you mean by believe, old man?" It was intended as an insult—Kaminsky and I were of the same age. "I'll tell you what I *couldn't* believe. I couldn't believe how easy you made it for me. You did everything I needed. I ought to thank you."

"Why me?"

"Why you? Why anyone? I needed a fall guy, and Captain Grobe was my *Schlemiel*. A perfect fit for the job. You did well, you created a masterpiece of confusion. And to make it all the more perfect, Captain Grobe is no mere van der Lubbe —he's a guardian of the establishment. I've no need to set the Reichstag on fire when I can use you to saw the legs off the Round Tables."

Kaminsky chuckled, amused by his own words. But the

smile soon dropped from his face. "You asked whether I believe? Don't you know I am the deliverer of our nation? I shall bring peace and prosperity to our GDR. I tell the people: trust me, put your faith in me, give me your power and you won't have to worry about anything. I love my country. I love the achievements of the last forty years and I'm not alone in that. There's a *Volk* out there, desperate to trust me."

Seeing that I was no longer paying any attention to what he was saying, Kaminsky headed to the door.

"You're history," I told him as he turned. "You're a ghost walking in the daylight."

"How poetic—the spectre of Communism! But I think you'll find you're the one who's a ghost. The slaughtered innocent haunting *our* party." Kaminsky paused at the door. "Face it Grobe, I've won. I'd already won before you even realised you were in the game."

Day 10
Tuesday
21st June 1994

Berlin: A suspect has been detained in the case of the murder of Hanna Krause. Police sources have indicated to Radio DDR I that the person is known to Berlin Kripo and is a member of a state agency.

08:00
Karo

I got really frustrated at the morning meeting: everyone was being so negative, and although I was desperate to tell everyone about my visit to Dmitri, I had to wait ages before it was my turn.

Klaus had nothing useful to report, Martin's neighbours hadn't noticed anything—nobody had even seen me, despite the fact I'd called round nearly every day last week.

Erika and Laura said that Martin's solicitor was sorting out a visiting order so that we could go and see him, and they had brought a pile of paperwork, but they were concentrating on the one file lying open before them.

"The police seem to think that Martin shot Hanna Krause by mistake, that he was aiming for Kaminsky," said Laura. "Their theory is that he was at the rally, he shot Hanna during the storm, and then passed the firearm to an accomplice. They haven't found any gun, neither at the scene, nor at his flat."

"So, have I got this straight?" Klaus reached over to take the file from Erika. "They are saying that Martin was in the middle of the rally, he took out a gun and shot Krause, nobody tried to stop him, nobody tried to hold him, not one of the tens of thousands of people there even saw him do it?"

"Bollocks, absolute bollocks! They're trying to frame him!" I blurted out, but nobody responded. Klaus was skimming the file and Erika was looking through the pile before her.

"The police have also said ..." she paused while she pulled out a piece of paper. "They said they can show the whole thing was planned. The ministry hasn't seen that evidence yet so Antje hasn't been able to tell us what it is. She's not convinced by the case against Martin but can't come out publicly until we have something concrete to prove the cops are making it all up."

"What about publicity and protests?" I asked.

"It's a bit delicate, don't you think?" Laura said. "This could seriously damage the image of the GDR—an officer of the RS being accused of terrorism. Whether or not Martin is released he'll be associated with this assassination attempt."

"But it's going to come out sooner or later anyway. We've got to do everything we can to get Martin out! Or are you worried that he may have done it? Seriously, none of you can believe that our Martin shot someone?"

"Of course we don't think Martin did it but we can't openly support him until we have hard evidence," answered Erika. "We're in the same boat as Antje."

"So you're more interested in being good RS officers than in saving Martin? Fuck RS! It's being wound up anyway, what have we got to lose? Or maybe you're looking forward to being transferred to the police? Do you think all this might damage your chances in department K1?"

"Karo, that's not how it is, as you well know!" Laura

retorted. "We're doing everything we can to help Martin, and if you want to be part of that effort then you'd better pipe down and stop making ridiculous accusations."

"OK, but I don't want to rule out protests in support of Martin. I want that to be an option."

"Fine. Shall we work out what to do next?"

"We still don't know what Martin was up to these last few weeks, we need to find that out first." said Klaus.

"Hang on. I've got something useful: Dmitri said that Martin was investigating a plot to shoot Kaminsky, he was working with that cop Steinlein, the one who got beaten up by the fash in March. And I saw them together, on Stralau, they were driving from the far end of the peninsular towards town. It was the night before the rally."

There was a suitable silence while everyone digested the news.

"OK, we should check that out—the whole Steinlein angle is our priority. We have to try to talk to him," said Erika.

"We need to be discreet about it. Steinlein won't want to be seen talking to us," said Laura. "I'll approach him when he's off duty."

"We'll do a bit of digging, if we can find out what Steinlein and Martin were doing together it may help you prepare your approach," agreed Erika. "Karo, do you want to do that with me?"

I nodded, but Laura had already chipped in with her next point: "I'm meeting Martin's solicitor this morning. I'll ask about the new evidence and try to have the remand order revoked."

"And what about publicity, and getting some protests happening?" I knew I wasn't making myself popular by banging on about this but I didn't want it to be forgotten.

"I think we should hold off for the moment, if for no other reason than to protect Martin. He may still be released before his arrest becomes public knowledge," said Laura. "How about we put it on the agenda to discuss tomorrow?"

Everyone agreed to that, except me.

"OK," I caved in. "But if that arsehole Kaminsky starts making political capital out of Martin's arrest then I'm going to make it my main mission to organise some demos."

09:17
Karo

"So this is where you saw them?"

I'd already told her twice and now Erika was asking me again. We were standing in front of the *Durchgangsheim*, Erika had a map in her hands.

"And they came from there?" she asked, pointing right.

"Erika, how many times? I was standing here, they came round that corner in a car." I took the map off her. "Why don't we just go and have a look what's round that bend?"

I had a look at the map, and saw why Erika was so confused. There wasn't anything much around the corner: a church, three shipyards, a few houses, a couple of other buildings and what looked like a park.

"Well, they won't have been at the shipyards, will they? So let's concentrate on those other buildings."

"Why have they got it in for Martin?" I wondered aloud while we walked towards the end of the peninsular.

"Bad luck, I guess. Martin always manages to be in the wrong place at the wrong time. But he'd probably say it's the other way round: that he's always in the right place."

I tried to grin at Erika's crap attempt at humour. "But this all seems so, I don't know, kinda random."

We'd passed the church and graveyard and the last residential house.

"Maybe it is random. But Kaminsky needs a scapegoat. He's been winding the whole country up for weeks, you know how tense it's become. Now he needs a trigger to make that tension spill over into action."

"So you think Kaminsky could have planned this?" Erika's theory reminded me of what Dmitri had said. Kaminsky was a real piece of shit, but would he gamble everything on something so risky?

"Framing Martin benefits Kaminsky," she replied.

We'd left the last boatyard behind, the clanging of hammers and the ring of tools faded. Calm descended—birds twittering, children playing—I could even hear the lapping of the river against the pilings. The kids that I'd heard were outside a building with lots of large windows. A woman, just a bit older than me, was keeping an eye on them.

"What's this place?" I asked her, trying to look friendly.

"We call it the Blue House. And what do we call yous?"

"We're looking for two men who were in this area last week." Erika showed the woman her RS pass.

The woman laughed. "Well, if yous are looking for men hanging around ye've come to the right place! Blue House is where us bargees hole up while we wait to go through West Berlin." She gestured at a couple of freighters that were moored up nearby, and then at another dozen or so on the far side of the peninsular. "We've been held up these last few weeks because the *Wessis* are playing silly buggers with the border checks. And afore you ask we can't get down the River Oder because water levels are low. So we're stuck hanging around here, just like the old days."

Erika poked a couple of photos under her nose, probably to shut her up.

"Who are they?"

"Have you ever seen either of these men?"

"That one's a cop!" the woman stabbed her finger at Steinlein's mugshot. "I saw him once in uniform, lots of silver and gold pips weighing down his shoulders. But usually he was just wearing normal clothes-"

"When did you see him?"

"I dunno, when did we arrive? Must have been Thursday,

yeah, Thursday because Willi was bringing his lighters over from the power station. I was stood here watching them come alongside when I saw that cop. Limping, had a cane. But as for that other one ..." She shook her head.

"Anyone here who might have seen this person?" Erika shuffled Martin's picture to the top.

"You'll be after asking old Henning. Goes to church twice a day, and wanders up and down the road when he's not on his knees. That's his boat, there, the push tug, keeps it nice and tidy, does our Henning-"

"Could you fetch Henning for us?"

Erika was being so patient, I would have totally lost it by now if I'd been asking the questions. But the woman was already heading into the Blue House, still talking: "You mind and keep an eye on those kids for me ..."

As soon as she was out of earshot I grabbed Erika's arm, shaking her with excitement.

"We're finally getting somewhere, we know Steinlein was here last Thursday!" I said to her.

"Don't get your hopes up too soon, we'll need a lot more than this to get Martin out. And until we do, we haven't got any hope of stopping Kaminsky."

Before I got totally depressed by Erika's über-realism this Henning guy appeared. He wasn't that old, maybe the same age as Martin or Erika, so definitely not quite ancient. He lumbered to a halt in front of us, and stood, waiting patiently for something to happen. At least it didn't look like he was going to blether on and on like the last person.

"We're wondering if anyone here saw either of these two men," said Erika holding out the photos of Martin and Steinlein.

"Aye."

"Which one?"

"That one first." He pointed at Martin's picture. "Looked beat up. Black eyes, bit of a limp. Thursday it were. Then the second one come out about ten minutes later. He had a limp too, worse than the other."

"Where?"

The man walked a few paces until he had a clear view down the road and pointed.

"That building there?" Erika asked.

The man nodded, waiting patiently for further questions.

"What were they doing in there?"

"How would I know a thing like that? Plenty of shouting, mind. Could hear them cussing and blinding from the road." Henning shook his head in disgust.

"Did you see either of them before Thursday?"

"Just that once. But if you ask Paule, he were here since the Monday of last week."

"Can we speak to Paule?"

"Ha! Only if yous are psychic."

Psychic? The way he said it made me think of sinking boats and drowning sailors, or maybe Steinlein ran amok with his service weapon. But it was more prosaic than that.

"Our Paule and his crew: long gone. Set off yesterday, they did. Tekkin' a load up to Eberswalde."

Erika got on the smoky Ikarus bus to the S-Bahn station. She'd be in Oranienburg in just over an hour, hopefully she'd manage to catch up with Paule's barge and get a statement from him. It definitely looked like Dmitri was right: Martin and Steinlein had been up to something. Which meant Steinlein should know what Martin was doing last week.

Steinlein was the key to this whole thing. But what part had he played? He was based out of Schottstrasse police station, same as Neumann, and that was where they'd charged Martin—was Steinlein involved in framing our friend?

I crossed the road to look at the weird little building that the bargee had pointed out. It was half pre-fab concrete, half old-build. Two rusty gates closed off the drive, one of the gateposts had a sign: *Council of Ministers of the GDR.* Weeds were growing through the concrete slabs of the driveway.

But the thing that I noticed was that some of the weeds were crushed, as if they'd been driven over.

I tried the gate, expecting it to be all creaky and squeally, but it swung open soundlessly. I had a look around: three doors, I checked the locks on each. I looked through the dusty window of the first door, I could see a hall and a flight of stairs. On one side was a metal cupboard, the doors hanging open, revealing empty shelves. There was nothing else to see. A look through the windows told me all the other rooms on the ground floor were just as empty, just some of those gormless portraits of Erich Honecker which suggested the building hadn't been used for over four years. But the crushed weeds told a different tale.

I was cycling away, heading towards Ostkreuz, trying to solve the riddle of the crushed grass when two cops waved to me from the side of the road. I looked around, no-one else about, they were definitely flagging me down.

I pulled into the kerb and put my hand into my pocket, reaching for my RS pass.

"What are you doing here, miss?" asked one.

"State business," I answered, showing them my RS pass.

The one that had spoken took my pass, looked at it then gave it back to me. As soon as I'd pulled the pass on them their arrogance had given way to confusion.

They took a few steps back and held a short, worried conference.

"Our apologies, miss, we've received reports of suspicious activity ... person answering your description." The cop touched his fingers to the peak of his cap, and I cycled on.

At the next corner I looked over my shoulder. One of the cops was holding his radio mike to his mouth, the other was staring after me.

"No grounds to detain them," the border guard said to the punk.

The border guard was Rico, and the punk was Tam. The punk lived on the *Lohmühle* trailer site just beyond the watchtower. I'd first met both of them in March when Tam was facilitating a meeting at which Rico was a reluctant participant. Now they were both looking through the gap in the Wall, watching two figures waiting to be cleared for entry by West Berlin police.

"Who you talking about?" I asked them.

"That's Giesler. Used to be a border guard under my command. Martin wanted to talk to him a few months back—that's when he and I first met."

"And the skin with him," added Tam, "used to be in my school. Steffen Huber. Nobody liked him, he never really fitted in. First of all he was a total communist, ultra-enthusiastic about being in the FDJ. Then he really got into all the militarist training crap with the GST. After 1989 he got involved with the skins. Feels a bit weird, seeing him again."

I looked across the bridge towards West Berlin, the two figures were heading towards Schlesisches Tor.

"Why did Martin want to talk to Giesler?"

"Gang of skinheads attacked a punk concert about six years ago. Giesler was a policeman at the time, and Martin wanted to ask a few questions. Doubt he got very far though," Rico answered.

Martin must have been interested in the attack at the Zion Church in 1987, which explained the old newspapers in his office. It was ancient history. Famous, but still ancient. What is it about Martin, he's always digging up the past as if he thinks the present isn't already hard enough.

I was about to suggest we head over to the watchtower for

a cup of coffee when a car pulled out of the little petrol station just over the border, thirty of forty metres inside West Berlin. As the car swung onto the road I could clearly see the driver.

"Fucking hell—that's Becker!" It was definitely him, I recognised him from the photo in his personnel files. I grabbed Rico's field glasses and focussed on the car. It stopped to pick up Giesler and Huber, then drove on. "Been looking for that man for months." I returned Rico's binoculars.

"And it looks like he knows our friend Giesler. Did you get the make and licence?"

"Er, it was red wasn't it?" I tried.

"Volkswagen Polo, West Berlin plates. Here, I'll write the number down for you." Rico scribbled in his pocketbook and tore the page out.

I crossed into West Berlin, for some reason the border checks had been relaxed and I didn't have to wait long before the cop on the other side of Wall waved me on. My task was to go and see Katrin, tell her about her dad. I guess I had to reassure her somehow that it was going to be OK (even though right now everything was the complete opposite of OK) and the closer I got to Katrin's flat the more I wished it wasn't me having to tell her. I wanted to see her, I really did, but was nervous about it, too. And I definitely wasn't looking forward to telling her about what was happening.

Maybe that was why I took the long way round and ended up cycling through Lausitzer Platz, which was a good thing. Because, there, parked by the church was a red Polo. There was a good chance that it wasn't the same one, I mean, have you seen the number of little red cars in West Berlin? I carried on to the next corner then got off my bike and tried to find the piece of paper Rico had given me. I squinted around the corner, yep, that was the car, sitting empty. What do I do now? I looked across the square, lots of people, sitting at tables outside cafés, cycling around, walking around. Becker and the others might even be somewhere close, on their way back to the car.

I decided I needed some camouflage. If I'd been in my half of town I would have just ordered a coffee at a café, but there was no chance of that over here in the West, I couldn't afford the prices. So I just sat down in the shade of a building and asked passers-by for spare change—it's what punks do most of the time over here—I fitted in perfectly.

I got a load of abuse and a few coins, and was just starting to think I might be able to afford that coffee after all when Becker came back to his car, followed by the skin, Huber. They were about twenty or thirty metres away, close enough to see clearly, but not close enough to hear what they said.

Huber stood behind Becker, who opened the car door and reached in to grab something. It was an envelope, one of those rough grey ones we use over in the East. It was folded over lengthwise and when Huber took it, he folded it again before sticking it in his pocket.

Becker got into the car and started the engine. I had a choice—follow Becker in the car or Huber who was now crossing the square on foot? I decided to go after Huber—I wanted Becker badly, but I didn't rate my chances of keeping up with him. Easier to follow someone who was on foot.

I unlocked my bike and went after Huber. He just loped along, not particularly bothered about anything at all. He crossed Skalitzer Strasse on a red light and the cars all beeped at him, but he just carried on. By the time I'd managed to cross he'd disappeared. I guessed he'd gone into Görli park, but when I went through the gates I saw I had no chance—everywhere I looked there were masses of people: hippies lounging around smoking pot, punks with ghetto blasters and Turkish families setting up barbecues. The place was packed. Literally packed. I'd lost the skinhead.

I was pissed off with myself, why hadn't I just run across the road instead of waiting for a gap in the traffic? Then again, I was in West Berlin for a reason, and I guess right now that was more of a priority than looking for Huber. And anyway, was it so surprising that Becker knew this skin? Becker was involved with the Nazis, and so was Huber. The only surprising bit was this Giesler that Rico said used to be a border guard. I'd mention it to Martin once we'd got him out of the nick.

I walked to Katrin's, still thinking about Huber. It was time to forget about Becker and the others, and start trying to work out how to tell Katrin about her dad. I rang her bell, and waited for ages but no-one answered. Maybe she wasn't in? I felt hopeful and despondent all at once. I rang the bell again and waited for even longer but finally I had to admit it.

Katrin wasn't home.

16:16
Karo

Some kind of wake was going on back at the offices, everyone was talking in low voices, passing round pieces of paper as if they were death notices.

"How are we getting on?" I decided a cheery note was in order.

But nobody reacted. I sat down at the table and took the evening newspaper that Klaus handed me.

"*Kaminsky in bid to abolish Round Tables*," I read the headline out loud. Now I knew why everyone was so down. It looked like Kaminsky was serious about wresting power from the Round Tables, and if he succeeded then it would be the end of the new-GDR, the end of direct grassroots involvement in running our country. It would stop our slow revolution dead.

Before I could react Klaus handed me a bundle of files and photographs.

"What's all this stuff?"

"Martin's solicitor got access to the initial evidence," Klaus replied.

They were statements by witnesses who saw Martin in an unstable state just outside the Soviet Memorial, immediately after Hanna Krause was shot.

"What's all that about? They're saying Martin was off his head? Do we believe that?" I asked

Nobody answered, so I looked at the next sheet. It was an analysis of fingerprints found on a Makarov pistol. Result: they were Martin's. Results of ballistic analysis of said Makarov: the pistol had been used in the murder of a police informant in April.

OK, this was getting unreal. I couldn't imagine Martin with a gun, never mind shooting anyone! Just not his style. Feeling queasy, I looked at the next load of papers. It was another mix of statements and photographs. I read the top statement, it was making out that Martin had contact with foreign agencies, subtext: Martin was a traitor.

"For fuck's sake! This can't be happening! There is no way, just no fucking way ..."

"Have a look at the photographs," Laura said.

I shuffled through them. Martin getting out of a Western car in front of some concrete flats; Martin shaking hands with a British army officer; a series of snaps showing Martin wearing shades and swimming trunks, looking the other way while a person approaches and picks up an envelope that's lying on the grass next to Martin. The camera's focus had remained on Martin, and the figure was blurred.

I was about to make some stupid comment about the photos when the envelope caught my eye. I couldn't be exactly sure—the photo was black and white, but it definitely looked like a grey envelope. It was A4, and looking at the next photo I could see the person who had taken the envelope was folding it lengthwise.

It was the way the envelope was being folded that had caught my attention. Becker gave Huber a grey envelope, just a couple of hours ago. Same size, same colour, folded lengthwise—not the way you or I would fold an A4 envelope, along the long side to make an A5 size. It was a standard, grey A4 envelope like millions of others. It couldn't really be the same envelope, despite the weird folding.

But the blurry figure photographed with Martin, I knew who that was. "That's Becker!"

I looked more closely at the other photos in the series, yep I was sure of it. I jumped up and went into my office, bringing Becker's file and photo back. I passed it around, and my colleagues compared Becker's portrait with the unclear figure in the photos.

"How can you tell? This figure in the photo with Martin is completely blurred, it's as if the photographer did it deliberately," said Klaus.

"I know it's him, I've seen him in real life, I followed him this afternoon. That's definitely him in the photo!" I quickly reported what had happened in Kreuzberg, how I'd seen Becker, Giesler and the skinhead Huber.

While I was speaking Laura went to the chalkboard. She wrote the three names and linked them with lines.

"We know that Martin has had contact with Steinlein recently—we've got two independent witnesses, plus Karo has confirmed it." She added Steinlein's name to the board. "Now we know he had contact with someone who may be Becker-"

"Not *may be*, it's deffo him! It's obviously him in the photo!"

"OK, let's assume for the time being that it's him. Now, if we believe the dates and times they say these photographs were taken then all of these meetings took place last week." Laura drew an arrow from Becker's name and wrote Martin next it. "We also know that Martin had contact with Steinlein several times last week." She wrote Steinlein and joined him to Martin with another line. "What do we need to find out?" she asked the room at large.

"What was Martin doing with Steinlein, did he know Becker, and did he know Becker was there? From the photo we can't tell whether he's deliberately looking away or whether he's completely unaware of Becker's presence," said Klaus.

"What about if we try to find out what Steinlein was doing on the days Martin met Becker—around the times the photos were taken?" suggested Erika.

"And why did Becker take that envelope from Martin, what was in it?"

"And is it the same envelope that Becker gave to Huber?"

"Where were the photographs taken, and by whom?"

They carried on coming up with questions and ideas while I looked through my notes on Becker. I couldn't see any links. Steinlein was a cop, always had been as far as I knew. Becker had worked for the Ministry of People's Education up to 1988, and sometime around or after 1989 he got involved with the fascists. I told the others what I was thinking.

"Go further back, where did Becker do his national service?"

I leafed through my scribbles again, wishing I'd been more systematic. My notes were all over the place, my thoughts, bits of stuff that Schimmel had told me, scrawls I'd added when I was in the Ministry for People's Education archive. And then, there it was: "Becker was a *Volkspolizei* auxiliary when he was a student in Köthen."

"Anything else? Who did he work with, what dates?" Klaus was already reaching for the phone.

I gave Klaus the dates, and we all sat waiting while he spoke to someone at Köthen police station. A few minutes later he hung up, a rare smile appearing under his moustache.

"Don't you just love these small towns where nothing ever happens? Can you believe it, the desk sergeant actually remembered Becker from twenty years ago? Apparently he was usually attached to work with a certain sergeant Neumann, who transferred to Berlin *Kripo* in 1977."

Klaus crossed over to the board, added Neumann, and drew a line from Neumann to Becker, and from Neumann to Steinlein.

"And there we have the missing piece of the puzzle," he announced.

We stared at the chalkboard, trying to get our heads round this new development. Martin was working with Steinlein. Steinlein answered to Neumann, who knew Becker. And I'd seen Becker hanging out with Giesler and the skin Huber.

"Who's heading up the investigation into Martin?" I didn't really need to ask, I could already guess.

"Neumann." Klaus went to the board again and drew a thick line between Neumann and Martin. Now a messy web linked almost every name to each of the others.

I stood in front of the board, looking at all the lines. This was good, we had opened up a whole new way at looking at what was happening. I wanted to kiss and hug my colleagues —we were finally getting somewhere. But before I could get too smug about it all I noticed Klaus frowning over the disclosure papers. The way he was pulling a face made me want to scream at him—we were finally getting somewhere but he was about to go all negative on us.

"Something's not right, it doesn't feel right." He had an outline map of the Soviet War Memorial on top of the other papers, his thumb was pressed against the barrow with the statue of the soldier on, his forefinger was pressed on the first oblong of grass. "Is that fifty metres? Would you say that's about fifty metres?"

I shrugged, but Laura was peering over Klaus' shoulder, her eyes measuring the distance between his thumb and finger.

"Makarov," said Klaus. "Great weapon. Simple, reliable, cheap to produce." Klaus was looking around, expecting us to take an interest in his gun fetish. "I trained with it during national service. Only problem with the Makarov is that it's not a precise weapon. Fifty metres, any more than that and you can't be sure of hitting your target."

"So?" I couldn't see what Klaus' point was, but he seemed excited about it.

"So, if Hanna Krause was shot by a Makarov then the shooter would have been standing in one of the first few rows of the crowd. I can't imagine anyone using a Makarov from further back." Klaus was staring at the map, finger pressed against where he imagined the assassin standing. "But it makes no sense—those first few rows would be where Kaminsky's biggest fans and his security were standing. If you fired a gun in Kaminsky's direction while you were in the middle of that lot—you wouldn't get out alive."

DAY 11
Wednesday
22nd June 1994

Berlin: The suspect in the case of the murder of Hanna Krause has been named. Unofficial sources have identified the alleged shooter as Martin Grobe, known for his activities as an officer of the controversial Republikschutz counter-intelligence agency.
Earlier today, Dr. Kaminsky, Member of the Volkskammer and General-Secretary of the PDS repeated his calls for an immediate dissolution of the RS: "The Central Round Table has no control over their own agency—it's out of control and, tragically, on Saturday Hanna Krause paid the price."

08:07
Karo

At the meeting this morning we checked on progress, and I talked about last night—it had gone really well, and I was dead chuffed about it. I told my colleagues about how, after leaving the office last night, I'd gone back to my own scene.

The first thing I did was go and see my best mate, although when I got there Schimmel didn't seem that pleased to see me. Trying to mend fences, I said sorry. Again.

"You told me to back off and I didn't. I should have listened to what you were saying."

Schimmel was sitting on the floor, staring into space. I

wasn't even sure he'd heard me apologise. "You go delving into my life, digging up my personal shit," he said. "It doesn't matter to you whether or not I'm OK with that. But if anyone ever asks you about your past you go ape. It's not on."

It was a rant, but it came out all mechanical, the whole time he was speaking he stared across the room. It was dead weird, and it made me feel really uncomfortable. Maybe it was just because he was right and I was finding it hard to face up to that fact.

"This is for you. Peace offering?" I gave him an envelope, one of those grey ones that had got Martin into trouble.

"What's in it?" Schimmel took the envelope, but didn't open it.

"It's what I've found out about Becker. There's a photo in there, and some biographical details. But I haven't managed to get hold of an up-to-date address."

Schimmel just shrugged and put the envelope on top of one of the computers that clutter up his room.

"I've kept a copy because we might need it to help Martin." I told him.

"Martin? What's he got to do with it?"

I told my friend what was happening to Martin, I thought he might be shocked, but he was more pissed off.

"How long have you known about this? And you're only just telling me now? Martin's a mate, which is more than can be said about you!" He lurched to his feet and ran down the stairs to the central kitchen. As I followed I could hear the gonging of the cymbal that hangs over the sink.

My ex-housemates began dribbling in. "What's up? What's the alarm?"

Schimmel told them about Martin. "We were there when he raided the Ministry of the Interior last year, and you know about when the fascists kidnapped him and we kicked their arses. Well, Martin needs our help again. The bastards are framing him for shooting Hanna Krause. He's on remand and nobody knows about it!"

They were making all the right noises so I just sat at the back and listened. They were talking about doing a demo outside the prison. Definitely sounded like a good start to me.

"C'mon you," said Schimmel after a while. He grabbed my hand and dragged me out of the kitchen. "Let's go and spread the word!"

We spent the evening going round all the squatted social centres to tell people about the demo. It was good to be with Schimmel again, and it was doing him good too—that evening was the first time for ages that I'd seen him actually look really alive.

"We need to speak to Martin, find out where he was standing at the rally," Erika said. "He might have seen something."

"I'll contact the solicitor again, find out how she's getting on with the visiting order," answered Laura.

It went on like that for ages, everyone coming up with things we needed to find out, do or discuss.

At some point I managed to escape and headed over to West Berlin. Rico wasn't on duty, but I got a salute as I passed through the border checkpoint.

I'd phoned Katrin, made sure she would be at home when I got there. Talk about uncomfortable—that was probably the worse phone call I've ever had—and all the worse for having Erika and the others in the same room.

So you can imagine how nervous I was when I rang Katrin's bell. I hadn't told her what I wanted to see her about, just that it was really urgent and really important—she probably thought I was planning to dump my heart at her feet and beg her to give me a chance.

But when I told her about Martin she went quiet.

"What are you doing about it?"

I told her everything. That we were working on getting

enough evidence to free Martin, that we were worried that if we didn't manage to do it soon then the other side would make up enough stuff for at least some of the charges stick.

"Who's the other side?"

"We don't know." I watched Katrin, she was dead still and her face was hard. "But we're pretty sure some cops are involved. A Lieutenant Steinlein and his superior, Captain Neumann. Probably others too."

"Cops? Some cops are framing my dad? That's insane! Why can't you just live in a normal country like the rest of us?" Katrin was really screwing herself up over this, and fair play, it was about her dad.

"And why are you only telling me now? Two whole days you've known about this! Why didn't you tell me as soon as you found out?" Katrin stopped pacing around, she stood there, hands on hips, storms of emotion marching across her face.

"That's my fault, I ..." I couldn't find a way to say it—my reasons for not hanging around yesterday, not waiting for Katrin to come home, not even phoning, they seemed so petty and useless now: because I was too embarrassed, heartbroken, proud.

Crap. Really crap reasons.

"Pick up the phone, that's all you had to do. Pick up the phone." Katrin had turned around, she was facing the other way. "I want you to go."

"We wanted to ask you, about getting word out, you know, in the newspapers, the radio—get it into the Western media-"

"Fine."

"We were thinking you might have some contacts, you know, through the work you do with AL?"

"I said, *fine*."

"What about the details? I need to-"

"I'll get them from RS. Just go."

I should have gone straight back to RS but I wanted a bit of time to think. Katrin was really upset, she had a right to be, I should have phoned her the moment I found out about Martin. I felt shit.

Again.

So far, this week was turning out to be even worse than last week. I didn't want to hang around the streets of Berlin, feeling sorry for myself, but I didn't want to go back to the office either. I just wasn't cut out for all the paperwork, the phone calls and working through all the bureaucracy. It was all necessary if we were going to get Martin out, but it didn't feel like *me*.

What I did last night, being with a gang of punks, getting fired up about injustice, being there when demos are organised, going on protests—that's what I do best, that's me.

Still, you do what you've got to do, and Martin's a friend, it's my job to help him. Solidarity. Right now that meant I should stop brooding and get back to RS.

While I was doing all this heavy thinking I'd been wandering the streets of Kreuzberg. I'd got as far as the Kotti. There were millions of people about, just like there always are, but one of them was a skinhead, patiently waiting for the traffic lights to change.

The skin was Steffen Huber.

Huber crossed the road and went straight past me, heading up Skalitzer Strasse. I followed him, watching him sway from one side of the pavement to the other, passers-by nervously dodging out of his way. What to do? I wanted to confront him, try to find out what was going on, but dealing with a pissed up skinhead didn't sound like such a great idea.

I followed him as far as Lausitzer Platz, just round the corner from where Katrin lives, and watched him go into a kebab shop. Maybe this was my chance after all.

I reckoned I had three minutes. I legged it to Katrin's and kept my finger on her bell until she buzzed me in.

"Katrin. Sorry, really, really sorry, but I need to borrow your tape recorder thingy. Just for ten minutes, quick! It's for Martin." I was puffing and panting from running and I must have looked desperate because Katrin didn't argue. She just got the recorder.

"Can you lend me five marks as well?"

She gave me the dosh, still without a word, her face tight. Before I'd even turned to go back down the stairs she'd shut her front door.

I ran back to the kebab shop. Huber was still in there, watching his döner being put together. I waited on the street, catching my breath and trying to look inconspicuous. I looked around, checking that nobody was paying too much attention, but in Berlin nobody really cares what you do or what you look like. Except, perhaps, for that woman in the red top on the other side of the square. When I first looked in her direction she'd been staring into the plate glass of an empty shop window. Didn't really notice her until it struck me how odd it was to spend so much time looking at an empty shop. I looked again, but she'd gone.

I was still trying to process it when Huber came out.

"Steffen, great to see you!"

Huber looked like he was about to tell me to fuck off, but I didn't give him time to do that.

"Listen, mate," I moved closer and lowered my voice, trying to come across all conspirational. "You did great work —absolutely fucking ace. Let me shake you by the hand."

He was looking confused now, unsure whether to punch me or to offer me his hand. His pupils were like black holes and he had a really bad case of red-eye. So not drunk, more stoned. Or both. This was perfect, almost too perfect.

"You know what, I'm going to buy you a beer. Least I can do after all you've done for the movement."

Huber puffed his chest out and stood up straight, not noticing his kebab was dripping on his boots. "Well, you know, it was nothing." Huber wasn't just beginning to relax, he was about to burst with self-satisfaction.

"I want to hear all about it—let's get that drink, come on." I took him to a bar with benches outside. "I'll go and sort the beers, you plonk yourself down there."

I poked my head through the door and signalled to the barman that I wanted two beers, then I clicked on Katrin's tape recorder and put it back in my pocket before heading to the table where Huber was waiting for me. The confused look had returned—his coupon was a picture—like he was trying to work out a difficult sum in his head.

"Who are you?" he asked.

I lowered my voice again. "I'm in disguise—I'm not really a punk."

Huber nodded, a smile of relief climbing onto his face. "Wow, undercover! That's so cool," he whispered, as if he'd never heard of anything so amazing.

I was starting to enjoy myself, but a voice in my head was warning me not to push it too far. The barman brought the beers and I waited until he'd disappeared before I spoke again.

"You celebrating? Too right, after what went down on Saturday." I didn't know if he'd been at Kaminsky's rally, but it was worth a try.

"It was amazing! I was up a tree, two hundred meters, there was a storm." He smacked a fist into the palm of his hand. "*Bam!* Piece of piss hitting that bitch." He smiled to himself and took a sip of beer. "Took her out, *no problemo*, same moment as the lightning struck. It was amazing."

Shit, I hadn't seen that one coming! This was way heavier than expected.

"No hassle from the cops?"

"Nah, the Corporal sorted out those losers!"

"Corporal? You mean Becker?"

Huber stared at me for a moment, the pride on his spotty face turning into something else, something like suspicion.

"The Corporal! *Everyone* knows the Corporal." He looked at his half eaten kebab, then back at me.

Oh shit, think fast! "I meant Giesler, yeah, Giesler," I tried, but it was too late. I'd fucked up.

Huber was still staring at his kebab is if it would tell him what to do. While he was waiting for an answer I got up, pushed my beer over to his side of the table and nabbed his glass.

"Listen mate, been a total honour, but got to head off ... you know, bit of a mission. Say hi to the Corporal for me!"

I headed off sharpish, pouring the beer into the gutter and putting Huber's glass into a paper bag.

13:53
Karo

I was buzzing when I got back to RS, but I had to be patient. Laura was on the phone and everyone shushed me when I tried to tell them what I'd just found out.

Laura finally got off the phone, a curl of a smile on her face, like a trout that's just been hooked.

"Two of us can go to see Martin this afternoon. There's a visiting order waiting in the director's office."

"We can go and see Martin? That's ace, c'mon, that's really brilliant!" But the others didn't share my enthusiasm.

So I told them all to pin their ears back and listen while I played them the tape of Huber's confession. I was almost as proud as the skin had been. Everyone heard Huber pretty much admitting that he'd shot Hanna Krause. Trouble is they didn't look as excited as I felt.

"What's the problem? Hanna Krause was taken out by this low-life who says he was up a tree, two hundred metres away. Look," I pulled the paper bag out of my rucksack, "I even got his fingerprints. This is evidence, this is going to get Martin off the hook!"

"It does confirm our suspicions that Hanna wasn't shot with a Makarov, the confession and the prints, however, can't be used," said Laura.

"What you talking about? This is pure gold! We know who did it and how he did it!" This wasn't exactly the celebratory atmosphere I'd been expecting.

"Karo, you made a secret recording and obtained prints of someone in West Berlin—a foreign country. Even if you'd done it over here it wouldn't be admissible—you're not a sworn in RS officer. What you've got there is hearsay, nothing more."

Did they always have to piss over everything I did?

My consolation prize was to go with Erika to see Martin. Before we went into the prison we stood in front of the scary gate, about five metres high and made of grey metal.

"I always hoped I'd never have to go in here," I told Erika.

"And I hoped I'd never have to come back," she replied.

I reckon she'd won that round. I wanted to ask her when she'd been inside, what it was like, but it wasn't the right time. Anyway, it was kind of hard to talk—drums, whistles and fireworks were going off all around us—it was dead loud. The Friedrichshain and Lichtenberg massives were out in force, all to show solidarity with our Martin. The banners were a bit rubbish but at least there were loads of them: *Set Martin Free*, that kind of thing. But the crappiest was probably: *Martin Grobe: People's Martyr*.

"You ready?" I asked Erika, but she was already on her way to the sentry box where a nervous screw was keeping an eye on the demo.

"You can't come in, not while that lot's here," he was telling her, and he started to look even more nervous when he saw me coming.

"I am Lieutenant Lang, and this is my colleague Frau Rengold. We are expected by the director." Erika was doing that determined thing again, the same as when we were at the ministry the other day.

"I'm sorry comrade Lieutenant, I have my orders-"

"Then use that phone of yours to get new orders!"

The guard used the internal phone, muttering something into it and waiting for a reply. Eventually he hung up.

"Someone is coming."

Erika didn't look very happy about that, but decided not to argue the toss. We waited a few more minutes before the grey gates scraped open. Five or six screws came out, truncheons at the ready, and they formed a line between us and the demonstrators.

My mates saw what was happening and must have thought we were being kettled because they surged forward to rescue us. I waved them back, and Erika and I disappeared through the gap in the gate.

On the other side a more senior screw was waiting for us.

"Comrade Lieutenant, Colleague Rengold, would you follow me?"

All this formal shit was getting boring, but Erika was already following the senior dude up some steps into a building.

We went up to the first floor and along a corridor to a door, helpfully marked *Direktor*. But before we could go in, another senior dude with even more silver on his shoulders came along.

"Comrade Lieutenant, the Director apologises that he isn't able to see you personally, but-"

"That's fine," said Erika in a tone sharp enough to cut through all this crap. "We only need the visiting order to see Captain Grobe."

"I'm afraid that won't be possible, you understand-"

"No, we *don't* understand! The visiting order, if you please comrade *Obermeister*!"

"Because of the current situation StVE Rummelsburg is in lockdown, it is impossible to visit any of the detainees." This *Obermeister* was hardcore, he'd just carried on as if Erika hadn't spoken.

"There's a handful of kids out there and you're in lockdown?" Erika sounded dead contemptuous, I was so impressed I didn't pull her up on calling my mates *kids*.

"Correct, comrade Lieutenant."

It went back and forth like that, and Erika was dead scary, but this dude wasn't budging a millimetre. The oberscrew accompanied us back downstairs and into the yard between the two sets of gates. There was the gate we'd come in through, and I guess the other went into the prison. There was even a watchtower and a load of screws holding truncheons. Unless somebody opened that second gate we had no chance of getting to see Martin. Even I had to admit defeat.

"Inform the Director that the Ministerial Committee will hear of this, comrade *Obermeister*," was Erika's parting shot as we were let back onto the street.

"Did you notice something in there?" asked Erika before all the punks came to ask us what was going on.

"They were dead jumpy?"

"Not just that, didn't you hear the noises from inside? Metal plates and cups being banged against bars—the prisoners know about the demonstration out here, they can hear it."

15:22

Karo

"What did Martin say? Did you get the information we need?" Laura demanded as we walked through the door.

"There was a noise demonstration going on outside, they used that as an excuse not to let us in," Erika replied.

"A demonstration? Outside the prison? Irresponsible!"

"It's not like they knew we were on our way to see Martin!" I snapped, stung by Laura's criticism. "We agreed it was time to make some noise—remember? So you're totally out of order saying my mates are irresponsible!"

"Stop it you two!" Erika shunted me away before Laura and I could get into a real argument. "Laura, take it easy—we're all getting a bit tired and stressed. And as for you, miss," Erika turned to me. "Stop winding Laura up. No, no," she made shushing motions with her hands, stopping me from answering back.

Which was the moment Klaus chose to come in. He went straight to the radio and turned it on.

After widespread unrest throughout the country the emergency bill proposed by the General-Secretary of the PDS, Dr. Karl Kaminsky, has been brought forward. The Volkskammer *will debate the bill to abolish the Round Tables and Workers' Councils on Friday. Dr. Kaminsky said in an interview earlier-*

"Fucking ace!" I shouted as Klaus switched off the news again. "There's so much protest going on that Kaminsky has had to change his plans! That's incredible!" I was really excited, but Laura just pulled a face.

"Perhaps you weren't listening properly, young lady. It means we have less than two days to get Martin released and to stop Kaminsky."

23:44

Martin

It was late when the hatch in the door rattled open. The cell light had been switched on, and darkness curtained the glass bricks in the outside wall.

I stood at the back of the cell, waiting for whoever it was to come through the door. I hadn't been let out for exercise today, so hadn't had spoken to any of the other prisoners. It was frustrating not knowing what was going on outside—I'd heard the noise of a demonstration but I didn't know what it was about.

When the door finally opened it revealed not the grey uniform of a prison warder, but *Volkspolizei* green. Steinlein eased into the cell, glancing behind himself as he did so. He threw a bundle of clothes onto the bed and held a finger to his lips.

"I've come to get you out. Put those on," he whispered. He saw my hesitation and pointed to the clothes on the bed. "Come on, we don't have much time!"

"I can't just leave."

"You can. If you ever want to get out of here then now is the time."

I looked at Steinlein, standing by the door, listening for the footsteps of the guard. Could I trust him? I'd trusted him this far and look where that had got me. But he'd come to get me, I couldn't afford not to go with him.

I pulled off my prison clothes and climbed into the civvies Steinlein had brought.

"How are you going to get me past the guards?"

"No time to explain, pull the hat lower. Now come on."

DAY 12
Thursday
23rd June 1994

Berlin: *The border between West Berlin and the Capital of the GDR has now been completely closed to all traffic. The West Berlin Senate announced the measures this morning, expressing concerns about continued civil unrest in the Capital of the GDR.*

10:30
Karo

Even though it was early the main kitchen at *Thaeri* was packed. It felt like the whole of Friedrichshain was there, and most of Prenzlauer Berg and Mitte too. People were feeling good about getting it together yesterday, pulling off a noise demo at the prison. Now they were talking about a march.

"What's the latest, Karo?"

I told them that we still hadn't been allowed to speak to Martin, and that we were worried about Kaminsky's next move.

"Listen, Karo, no disrespect, and I know you're involved in this RS stuff, and so is Martin. But Martin's a good guy, heart in the right place—you know what I'm saying? So if he's in the can then I'll do my bit to get him out. But the Round Tables? Are they really that great? It's just a load of old men talking. There's no space for any of us there! What have the

Round Tables ever done for us?"

"Have you ever been to one?" I asked. "Have you ever actually contributed? At any level? You ever checked out the Neighbourhood Round Table? Maybe it is full of old men talking, but if they're the only ones who bother turning up then what do you expect? The tools are only as good as the people using them!"

"Yeah, but it's not really our scene, is it?" someone else offered.

"Fuck's sake! What do you mean it's not our scene? This is where you live, and you say the neighbourhood RT isn't your scene? Four years we've been at this, four years! It's no wonder people are saying that it's not working! If not even people like us can be bothered to get involved then it's not going to fucking work, is it?"

"Easy Karo, we do our bit! Look at all that stuff that went down in spring, we dealt with the fash, didn't we? Without us none of that would've happened."

"It's not enough! How can that be enough? We're not just needed when something really major goes wrong. It's not enough to just turn up whenever there's a sexy action or a fuck-off demo being planned!" I realised I was shouting, but by now I didn't care. "If we don't think the Round Tables are doing the right things then we need to get involved and not just fucking moan about it."

"You know what Karo, again, no disrespect, but maybe you've been hanging out with that lot from the RS too much. Institutionalised, that's what you sound like."

"Fuck you, fuck the lot of you!" I left them to it, lazy fucking shits. It was like they *wanted* Kaminsky to centralise all the power again so that they could blame somebody else when things got worse.

I stood on the doorstep, feeling absolutely fucked off. *Deep breath, Karo* I told myself, *deep breath.* I needed to stick to the script. Twenty-four hours to get Martin out and stop

Kaminsky from trashing everything we've achieved since 1989. I was about to get on my bike when I heard the door open behind me. I turned around, ready to take a bite out of whoever it was. But it was Tam.

"Do you remember back in March, when you came to that meeting at the *Lohmühle*?" she said. "We decided to open up a new border crossing. You weren't sure about working with the local Round Table either. None of us that night thought it would work. Except Rico, maybe." Tam broke off to give me a shy smile. "But we did it, and it's working out. It's hard work dealing with all these other people when the only thing you've got in common is that you happen to live in the same neighbourhood. But it can work."

"Yeah, well, we don't have to worry about that for much longer, Kaminsky will have got rid of the Round Tables by this time tomorrow."

"The point I was trying to make is that all this is scary. It's scary to take responsibility, to open yourself up to other people. Maybe it's just," Tam looked over her shoulder to where the front door of *Thaeri* still stood open, "maybe they're more scared than lazy."

"So why don't you go and talk to them about it? No point telling me, is there?" I was being mean now, but I was still pissed off by my ex-housemates and all the other losers who think they're so radical but can't actually be arsed doing anything about it.

"What's your next step?" Tam asked.

"I want to get some demos and stuff happening tomorrow, outside the Palace of the Republic while the debate is going on. Let parliament know that we're not going to give up our Round Tables and Workers' Councils without a fight."

"OK, leave it with me. I know everyone from *Wagenburg Lohmühle* will be up for that. I'll talk to the Alt-Treptow neighbourhood Round Table, see if we can spread the word that way too. Don't worry, we'll get it sorted."

I got on my bike and cycled down the hill, feeling better after the chat with Tam, and maybe that's why I wasn't paying enough attention. Before I'd even noticed what was happening I had a cop car on my left and a Barkas van behind me. The car at my side accelerated and pulled across the roadway in front of me. I was pulled off my bike and shoved into the back of the van. Bastards didn't even let me lock my bike up.

11:07
Karo

The van stopped and I was pulled out of the back. They'd put handcuffs on me and, unable to steady myself, I nearly fell to the ground as I was dragged down the steps.

Watch out, you pigs! I wasn't stupid enough to say it aloud, but I definitely shouted it inside my head.

I had a cop on either side of me, they were deliberately trying to hurt me, one shoving me, the other pulling me by the wrists. I tried to keep my cool, tried to keep breathing. They just wanted me to kick off, they wanted me to scream and try to escape, any excuse to get their batons out and lay into me. Fucking pigs.

They shoved and dragged me into the police station. I recognised it, I'd been here before: Marchlewskistrasse. This lot thought they were well hard, the cocks o' Berlin. They had something to prove, and I was determined not to let them use me to prove themselves on.

I'd spent the time in the back of the van doing some thinking. There was too much at stake, I couldn't afford to let them keep hold of me—I had to get out, and fast.

We'd reached the custody officer, sitting all comfortable behind his desk. One of the cops had shifted his grip, he now held my arm, thumb jabbing painfully into my armpit, his knuckles resting against my left breast. He was deliberately moving his fingers back and forth and he was getting off on rubbing against me. I was going to get this fucker, I was going to memorise his face and track him down.

"Name and reason for detention?" demanded the custody sergeant. He hadn't even looked up, just had a pen in his hand, ready to fill in the form.

"Rengold, Karoline. Detained in execution of an arrest warrant," said the perv on my left.

"Authority issuing warrant?" asked the sergeant, bored.

Perv and his copper mate exchanged a look. They didn't have the details, someone else had requested the pick up.

This was it. Deep breath, keep calm. Don't protest, sound authoritative. I straightened my spine, making myself as tall as I could. I looked at the top of the custody sergeant's head and willed him to look up. "There is no warrant, comrade Sergeant."

The sergeant looked up, then did a double take when he clocked my appearance—my punk outfit didn't match the voice I'd just used on him.

"Contact Captain Neumann from Lichtenberg K1 to confirm. And in the meantime take these cuffs off, I need the toilet," I said, still using the voice.

The sergeant looked from one of my guards to the other, his eyes demanding answers. Perv had taken his hand off me and had shifted away slightly, as if disowning me.

"The signal came from Lichtenberg, comrade Sergeant," said the other cop, not sounding too sure of himself.

"Escort Miss Rengold to the toilet," the sergeant barked.

Perv stood to one side, watching as his colleague released my wrists and took me down a corridor. Behind me I heard the sergeant pick up the phone.

Prisoners have buckets in their cells, and since I didn't have a cell yet I was taken to the staff toilets. I had no plan, no idea what to do next—but I'd bought myself a few minutes and hoped that I'd think of something.

"Be quick about it," my guard ordered, unwilling to give up his authority over me.

As I walked into the toilets my heart leapt. I was in the female locker room, the toilets themselves were through another doorway. I tried the first locker, civvy clothes, magazines, hairbrush. On to the next one, traffic cop uniform, that'd do. I pulled on the white blouson, the uncomfortable green skirt and the stupid, stiff white hat. Into the toilets, check in the mirror, push my hair under the cap. Now it looked like I had a skinhead, but that was better than a red mohican.

I pulled open the window, it wasn't barred because it let out into the inner yard and not the street outside. Fine, poke my head out, no-one in sight. Hopefully nobody was looking out of any of the windows either. One leg over the sill, then the next. Jump down to the concrete a metre or so below, then march over to the gate. *March* I told myself, don't slouch, don't run. Look like you're a cop, think like a cop. *Be a cop.*

12:57
Karo

"Maybe we've made a bit of progress in getting Martin out, but we're not even close to stopping Kaminsky," I was having a go at my RS colleagues again. "We haven't even got a proper plan yet! Oh, sorry, no. We have a plan: get Martin out and that will somehow magically be enough to stop Kaminsky. Super. Brilliant. Fan*fucking*tastic."

"The two are related, as you are well aware." Maybe I was giving them a hard time, but Laura could give as good as she got. "And as you also know, we thought we had a few weeks to deal with the situation."

"So, Kaminsky moved the goalposts. And now it looks like he's after us. Didn't you see me march in here wearing a copper's uniform? Didn't you hear me tell you I'd just escaped from police custody? We have to act. Like now—so what are we waiting for?"

"Karo's right," said Erika. "We need to adjust our plans. They're coming for us, we have to act now, before they arrest us all. We need something concrete against Kaminsky, something that will discredit him, show how he's been manipulating the situation to make sure his bill is passed."

Klaus and Laura were giving each other meaningful looks, it was like they blamed me for the situation we were in.

"I don't think they'll try to arrest us here, at least not yet, but no-one should leave this office alone. We always go around in pairs. Anyone not in this office should check in every hour. That way if one of us is arrested we'll know and can try to do something about it." Erika had taken over, she had a plan. "Laura, can you contact Antje and see about getting Karo's arrest warrant revoked? And check whether warrants have been issued for the rest of us. Then you and Klaus can carry on working on Martin's release, or at least get us a visit. Karo and I will dig a bit deeper, work on these possible connections between Kaminsky, Becker and Giesler."

"What about the skinhead? He practically admitted he shot Hanna," I was still proud that I'd found Huber.

"If we had more time we could work on that angle, but we don't have much to go on," Klaus joined in the conversation. "Kaminsky is our priority now, and there's no obvious link between Kaminsky and Huber. I think we need to let Steffen Huber go for the moment, he's a small cog and he's holed up in West Berlin where we can't reach him anyway. We'll pass his name to the prosecutor once we've dealt with Kaminsky."

Now we were starting to get somewhere—still too much talking, but at least we were making some solid plans. But it all came to a grinding halt when Grit poked her head round the door.

"Just had a call from *Ministerin* Willehardt's secretary, it's bad news. I passed on Klaus's query about where Martin was

183

standing at the rally, and whether he was close enough to have used a Makarov on Kaminsky and the others. Apparently the *Ministerin* asked the police for clarification and it took them over a day to get back to her. Now they're saying there was a mistake in the autopsy report, that she was killed by a ..." Grit checked her notes, "a soft nose 7.62×54 mm. They've found the casing of a bullet of that type with Martin's prints on it."

"Dragunov rifle," Klaus whispered.

"There's more: Martin's escaped, just heard it on the radio. He's on the run."

"Come on, it's not all bad news! They're obviously fabricating evidence against him, I mean, it's so bleeding obvious, first it was a pistol, now it's a rifle. They can't even get their own story straight. And now Martin's escaped— that's ace! First I get away from the cops and now Martin has too—go Martin!" This was exciting, this was the best news all week!

Except the others weren't excited. They looked pretty flabbergasted. Everyone's eyes and mouths were so wide open that they all looked like goldfish. Except Erika, who was holding her hand in front of her mouth, and goldfish don't have hands.

"Karo," said Laura after a moment. She used that patronising tone of voice that made me boil, "This is very bad news. This is going to make it easier for them—the focus now is going to be on Martin, they've got evidence against him, but if he's gone underground then he can't help us to prove he's been framed."

"Is this a bad time?" A quiet voice came from behind Grit.

Schimmel edged around the door, one hand clamped to the frame, the other fidgeting with the zip of his hoodie.

"We're rather busy at the moment-" started Laura, but Erika interrupted.

"Is it important, Schimmel?" she asked him, but from his face it was obvious that it was important.

"It's OK, I've got this, you carry on." I took Schimmel into my office, sat him down and listened to what he had to say.

"I looked at that stuff in the envelope, your research on Becker. I didn't want to look, but it felt stupid ignoring it. Is Becker," Schimmel swallowed, his eyes met mine for a second, then he looked down at his feet. "Is Becker really involved in framing Martin?"

"We're pretty sure he is." I was looking towards the door, wanting to get back to the others, but Schimmel needed to talk.

"Karo, you've been telling me for months that I need to move on, and I've just been a total pain in the arse, haven't I?"

"And you kept telling me to back off, but I didn't. Sorry."

Schimmel gave me a smile for that, then his head dropped down again. He was trying to work up the courage to say something difficult.

"You're right Karo, I need to move on. There's other stuff I need to be doing, and Becker's already fucked up my life once, I'm not going to let him do it again." Schimmel's face moved up until his eyes met mine. "If we get Martin out, if we stop Kaminsky, if we save the Round Tables and all of that—then Becker's lost hasn't he?"

"Haven't you heard? Martin's on the run, he broke out last night. Now it's all or nothing. We need to clear Martin's name and stop Kaminsky from destroying the Round Tables."

Schimmel did the same goldfish impression as the others. "I want to do my bit, I need to do my bit. Tell me what to do."

"Can you ring some Round Tables and Workers' Councils, see whether they're doing anything about Kaminsky's bill? If they're not, put them in touch with the nearest Round Table that is. We've got to mobilise them all, even if they just have a big meeting or something, it's got to be better than letting

Kaminsky stomp all over them."

"I can do that." Schimmel actually sounded excited. "What about Martin?"

"I don't know. We've only just found out about it. Listen, make a start and I'll be back in a bit."

"What do I tell them—shall I say I'm from RS?"

I hesitated—I should have asked the others, but fuck it, we didn't have time for stupid questions like that. "Tell them you're ringing from RS."

I went back to Erika's office. She was adding names and arrows to a big piece of paper on the wall.

"What's going on?" I asked her.

"We're making a list of people Martin might contact. He's going to need help, so the chances are he'll get in touch with someone."

"Be serious! We've already done all this names and arrows and lines shit, and it didn't help. Let's just *do* something. I mean, if Martin's going to get hold of us then he will, a list of names on your wall isn't going to change that, is it?"

"What do you have in mind?" Klaus asked.

"I think we need to be a bit more radical."

"Ye-es." Erika said. I could see they were all getting a bit jumpy now, preparing themselves in case I came up with something *too* radical.

"OK, the only workable theory we've got is the one linking Becker and Giesler with Neumann and Steinlein. But we can't chase up the Becker-Giesler-Huber bit of the equation without Martin's help. So if we can't talk to Martin then we should go back to where it all started."

"What do you mean?" Klaus was leaning forward now, elbows on the table.

"Look, the way I see it, Steinlein and Neumann are cops. They probably produce nearly as much paperwork as we do, and an operation like this with Steinlein working in the field and Neumann behind his desk, I'm guessing they've sent about a hundred memos to each other."

"Well that's for the public prosecutor-" said Laura but I ignored her.

"Here's the plan: we break into Neumann's office."

I sat down, wondering how they'd react. To their credit they didn't just say no, they sat there and looked at each other and had a think.

"I know you're going to say no." I couldn't bear the silence any longer. "If anyone's got another plan then I'm all ears, but at least think about-"

"OK," said Laura.

"OK? Did you just say OK?"

"I said OK. Let's hear more about this plan of yours, but you'd better make sure it's a good one."

22:17
Karo

The three of us were standing in the bushes outside the church on Roedeliusplatz, and even at this distance we could hear the demo outside Magdalenenstrasse prison.

"C'mon you lazy gits!" I murmured. The cops were taking their time—the demo had been going on for at least ten minutes already but not a single squad had left Schottstrasse police station.

"Here they come," Erika sounded excited, and who could blame her? "And another lot—three lorries. Great, the police station should be practically empty."

We waited for the trucks to disappear, one down the hill to the Magda prison, the others heading west to Rathaus Lichtenberg where the local Round Table was demonstrating against Kaminsky's bill.

"They were tooled up, did you see them?" asked Schimmel. "They're ready for a fight."

Nobody answered, I think we were all trying hard not to

think about what might be happening at the demos. The only thing we could do was to carry out our plan. And so far it was working: we'd organised the demo outside Magda prison and roped our mates into coming along. The Round Table demo outside Lichtenberg Town Hall was lucky coincidence.

"OK, Laura's here, she's going in. Now it's our turn."

We legged across the road, trying not to trip over the buckets and mops we were carrying. I had to giggle at the sight of Schimmel, wearing a dress and a nylon pinny, a scarf covering his spiky hair. His lean body and face had an androgynous quality; he suited his disguise. Erika and I had the same get-up, but somehow I didn't find it half as funny.

We entered the police station, moving with self-assurance past the front desk where Laura was playing a bothersome neighbour complaining about the noise from the demo down the road. She was giving the desk officer a hard time, not letting him get a word in edgeways. I think she was enjoying her role.

I guided my cleaning posse through the glass doors towards the back of the building where the *Kripo* had their offices. The whole place felt deserted, the *Kripo* had long since gone home, and the uniformed officers were out hassling demonstrators. I was whistling, starting to relax, actually looking forward to the task ahead. Down one corridor, through a door on to the next. Except a cop was there, coming towards us. A shove in my back, and I realised I'd stopped dead. I'd stopped whistling too, shock rooting me to the scuffed lino. Another shove, and my limbs mobilised. The three of us shuffled past the cop, who didn't even register our presence. A door swung shut behind us and he was gone.

"Fuck!" I breathed.

"C'mon, no big surprise," whispered Schimmel in my ear. "Just a cop in a cop shop. But be careful, we may find a typewriter in one of the offices—they can be really scary!"

I appreciated Schimmel's attempt to bolster my confidence, and just a few paces later I stopped outside Neumann's office. "This is us, time to do your magic."

Schimmel took a key wallet out of his pocket, opening it up and taking a couple of picks out as he dropped to his knees. Erika and I went to either end of the corridor to keep an eye open for any intruders.

I stood there, holding a mop across my body, listening to my pulse booming in my ears. It was so loud that I was sure I wouldn't hear anyone approaching. I was there for ages, concentrating on the door at the end of the next corridor, hoping no-one would come, wondering what I'd say if they did.

"Psst!" Schimmel had cracked the lock, and Erika and I scurried into Neumann's office. We shut the door behind us and let our eyes take everything in. The desk with a glass ashtray on it, a lamp, a blotter. Window opposite us, floor to ceiling cupboards covering one wall, Party and *Volkspolizei* pennants and certificates on the other.

Schimmel closed the curtains and turned the light on, then moved back to the door, gazing at us expectantly.

"You take the drawers, I'll do the cupboards," suggested Erika.

I tried the first drawer, locked. I gestured Schimmel over and he got to work while I took his place next to the door. It was a small office and there wasn't anywhere else to stand.

Erika had a cupboard open, revealing a rack of uniforms and a set of shelves full of ring-binders. She was patting down the pockets of a uniform jacket when I heard footsteps in the corridor outside. I flipped the light off and held my breath.

I could hear the tapping of feet on lino and the grumble of two men talking. The noises grew louder and clearer as they approached, punctuated by the rattle of door handles.

With a single stride I reached Erika, her shadowy form

just visible in the dim light leaking through the threadbare curtains. I pushed her into the cupboard, pulling the doors shut as I followed her in. The last thing I saw through the narrowing gap was Schimmel disappearing into the knee hole of the desk.

The cupboard was tiny. Every time I breathed in I could feel the door shudder outwards a fraction. I tried not to let the dust tickle my nose, or to let the smell of Erika's perfume scratch at the back of my throat.

"The Captain's left his door open—that's not like him." The two voices were in the office now, they'd switched the light on and must have been standing less than a metre away from us. I had to press my face into one of Neumann's uniforms to stop myself from giggling with nervousness. Stale smoke and body odour filled my nostrils. I was going to gag.

"You sure it was here that you saw the cleaning ladies?" The voice droned on, but the door had shut now. The lock clicked and the footsteps receded.

Schimmel was back on his knees, working on getting the door unlocked again. Every so often I could hear a scratching noise and an almost silent *shit!*

While he did that, Erika and I were hard at work, but we were getting nowhere. Nothing interesting, just admin crap like duty rosters and sheaves of impenetrable statistics.

"Woot! I got it!" The lock finally clicked and Schimmel got up and swung the office door open. "Ta-da!"

"Oh fuck!" I said it under my breath, but Schimmel heard me. His eyes swivelled in my direction, not understanding what my problem was.

My problem was standing in the doorway, just behind Schimmel.

My problem was a cop named Steinlein.

Karo

"You've got to be kidding!"

"Not now, Karo," snapped Erika. She was getting to be as catty as Laura.

I wasn't happy about being brought to this flat in Hohenschönhausen. In fact, the only reason I was here was because Steinlein had threatened to arrest me and bring me here in cuffs if I refused. I wished he had just let me go, like he had Schimmel.

"*Dobryi vyechyer.*"

"You too, Dmitri." Erika stood erect, breathing easily, refusing to return Dmitri's oily smile. She wasn't going to take any shit off this suave KGB officer. "What's going on?" She was looking at Dmitri but the question was meant for Steinlein.

"The comrade Captain would like to help you."

"You're going to help us? How?" I demanded of Dmitri. "You got some secret plans up your secret sleeves?"

"I'd like nothing more than to help." Dmitri turned his greasy smile on me. "But I'm sure you know there's not much I can do. What would you like me to do? Shall I surround the *Volkskammer* with Alpha Group troops? This is not Russia, and I am not Boris Nikolayevich Yeltsin."

"So what's the point of you?"

I was being rude, but Erika didn't stop me, so I reckoned she was as unhappy about the situation as I was. Then again she may have been distracted by the arrival of yet another person.

"Who's that?" I asked, but nobody answered.

I didn't know her, how could I? I'd never seen her in my life, but it felt as if I should know her, and that I should dislike her. She was attractive in a conventional sense, and she knew it. She was the kind of person that would think nothing of using her forget-me-not eyes and her killer smile to get whatever she was after.

"Karo," another smile from Dmitri, "allow me to introduce an old friend: Evelyn Hagenow."

"You must be Karo?" It wasn't a question, it was a statement, smiled at me by Evelyn.

I threw her the most vicious look I had.

"You're the one who came to ask my comrades for help when Martin went missing last March?" Another statement. "How brave of you. That's what real friends are for, and I do hope we will also be friends. After all, we have someone in common." She still hadn't switched off the smile, and it was irritating the fuck out of me.

"What do you want?" Erika's voice made it plain what she thought about Evelyn.

"And you're Erika?" The smile hadn't diminished a single watt, she was still beaming away. We were all at a diplomatic reception and she was the gracious hostess. "Martin told me so much about you, he has a great deal of respect for you."

"Perhaps you could get to the point?" Erika's tone was as icy as Evelyn's was false.

Evelyn wasn't at all flustered by the animosity we were chucking her way, she just danced around the room, wafting her perfume around, picking up ornaments and putting them back, trailing her hands over Dmitri and Steinlein when she swept past them. Evelyn was making sure she was the centre of attention, and I was busy wrinkling my nose at the transparency of her act when a thought struck me.

"Have you been following me?"

Evelyn floated over to the table, focussing on me. She was still smiling, but her eyes were no longer doing that flirty thing. "You were very helpful."

"What do you mean?"

But Evelyn's gaze had flicked towards Erika and her eyes softened again. "I have something for you. Or Martin. Yes, let's say it's for Martin, because once again it's about our dear friend." She took a file out of her handbag and placed it on the coffee table.

I stepped forward, reaching across the table, but Evelyn saw me coming, she placed her fingers on the grey folder and shook her head.

"Patience. You'll get the file, but first, let's be civilised. Please, sit down. We'll have a little chat."

Erika sat on the sofa opposite Evelyn and I sat next to her. Dmitri remained standing and Steinlein had moved over to the window. He had pushed the mint-green curtains apart to keep an eye on the road, but was actually taking more of an interest in what was going on in the room.

"Where have you been since March?" Erika broke the ice.

"Oh, here and there, working on a case. Truth be told, being on the run wasn't as much fun as I thought it would be. But I kept myself busy, had a few agents that needed looking after."

"You've been running agents? Here in the GDR?" Erika's voice had cooled even further, it was now well below freezing.

Evelyn gave one of her smiles and held up a hand. "Yes, here in the GDR. But hear me out before you jump to conclusions." She gave Erika a chance to nod. "I've been after Kaminsky for a long time. Operation WITHERED VINE was the reason I was so keen to help out earlier this year when you had your little problem with the fascists."

"Always helping, that's you, isn't it, you Stasi sow!" How could I not call her out on her fucking hypocrisy?

Evelyn shifted her attention from Erika back to me, a searchlight on full beam swept along the sofa.

"I had my own agenda, it's true. But I'm sure we agree on what we think about the fascists." The spotlight shifted back to Erika. "Kaminsky and the far-right have been in bed together for a long time—it's not just a recent thing."

"What's in it for the far-right?" Erika was hooked, but I was still sceptical.

"Power. What else is there?" Evelyn was no longer smiling, she was serious, her eyes narrowing in concentration. "Kaminsky did a deal with the leaders of all the larger far-right parties and groups. If they help him into power then he'll give them positions in his government."

"What kind of help?"

"Well, I assume even you amateurs know about the skins stewarding Kaminsky's marches and rallies, intimidating counter-demonstrators, that sort of thing?"

"We don't have to take this shit," I told Erika, but she just nodded at Evelyn, letting her know she should continue.

"It goes further, much further than oppressing the proles. Kaminsky climbed the Party ladder by bullying and threatening anyone who might oppose him. And guess who did the threatening part? Once Kaminsky gets his bill passed and disbands the Round Tables he'll move on to the next target: the other political parties. He's got dirt on all the major CDU and SPD politicians and he can terrify the smaller parties and the grassroots with his skinhead shock troops. By election-time in October Kaminsky will be the only one still standing."

Evelyn was painting a much bleaker picture than any of us had even begun to imagine: in the space of a few months Kaminsky intended to take our country back to a pseudo-democracy with all the strings in his hands.

"Some senior figures in the Party tried to stop Kaminsky, there was some talk of special operative measures, but they didn't even have the balls to come up with a proper plan, never mind carry it out. And anyway, the Party likes the idea of being back in power."

"Wait!" Steinlein had stopped even pretending to peer through the curtains and was now standing next to Evelyn. "Are you saying the Party never meant to assassinate

Kaminsky? What about the attempt on his life at the rally."

"That was Kaminsky's plan—a fascist cell carried it out. He got rid of a major opponent, and now he's playing the martyr card and blaming the government for their inability to keep the peace."

All the colour had drained out of Steinlein's face. He slumped onto a chair next to Evelyn and she placed a hand on his knee.

"Oh, sweetie. Bit of a shock, isn't it? There's never a good time to find out you've been played, is there? You and Martin did everything exactly as Kaminsky planned."

I wanted to ask Steinlein what he and Martin had been up to, but Erika put her hand on my arm, silencing me.

"Do you know where Martin is?"

Instead of answering, Evelyn turned to Steinlein who had now slumped even further down the couch.

"I tried to get him out last night. I failed," he mumbled. "I got away but they caught Martin. He's still in custody, they'll have him in solitary."

I had a million questions, but Erika's hand was still on my arm, and she tightened her grip briefly, telling me to hold my tongue.

"Why was Hanna at the rally?" she asked.

"Blackmail. Before 1989, Hanna's son was an informant for our lot," answered Evelyn. "He reported on the peace movement for years. Kaminsky found out and told Krause that he'd make sure everyone found out about her son's involvement with the Firm unless she endorsed Kaminsky at the rally. An impossible situation—whatever she did she'd lose her credibility. I suppose she hoped to at least save her son from being outed."

"And I presume you have evidence of Kaminsky and the fascists working together?"

"It's all here," Evelyn said, tapping her long fingers on her Get Out Of Jail Free card. "I must say young Karo was very helpful, it's thanks to her that we found out about Becker and Huber. We did a bit of digging and we're satisfied there's enough evidence for a prosecution."

"So you were following me?" I was getting really pissed off now, half rising from the sofa, but Erika still had her hand on my arm and pulled me back down.

Meanwhile, Steinlein was watching what was happening with greedy eyes, his gaze constantly flicking back to the file on the table.

"You can have the file, but first we need to negotiate. If the authorities get their hands on me I'll end up in prison again." Evelyn fixed her baby-blues on Erika. "I need a new identity, new papers. Sort that out and I'll go into retirement, make a new life far from Berlin. Would Thuringia be far enough for you? Or maybe the Baltic coast?"

"Why don't you get your friends in the KGB to give you a new identity, you can go and live in Russia!" Her demands were making me even angrier.

"You know, young Karo, I think you and I have a lot in common. Why are you still in the GDR? Why haven't you left? You could go West: Spain, France, America—world's your oyster. But you're still here. Why? Because you want to make a difference. You belong here, in the GDR. Just as I do— I belong, and I won't go into exile, not to Russia, nor anywhere else."

"You can't be trusted," I threw back. "If we let you stay in the GDR you'll just carry on working to overthrow this grassroots democracy we're building."

Evelyn did her false laugh again, looking around at the men, checking for their approval. "Yes, I'll carry on working against the fascists, but to be honest, they're a spent force. If Kaminsky weren't supporting them they'd have splintered and disbanded by now. As for your Round Tables, if Kaminsky doesn't manage to get his bill through tomorrow then they'll be unstoppable. As dear Dmitri never tires of saying," she beamed in his direction, "decentralisation is the best defence against power grabs from the likes of me and my Chekist friends."

"You know we can't provide you with a new identity." Erika said as Dmitri bowed his head in acknowledgement of Evelyn's words.

"Naturally. However, you do know the right people," Evelyn shifted her attention back to Erika and Dmitri was left in the shadows again. "You know people who can organise a new life for me."

Erika nodded, thinking about Evelyn's offer. After a while she turned to Dmitri.

"Have you seen this file? Does it have what we need?"

"I've seen it." Dmitri held his hands out, embracing the whole room, grateful to be at the centre of it all, if just for a moment. "There are one or two gaps, a few empty spaces on the stage, that's to be expected in a case like this. But there's enough in there: photographs, phone records and transcripts. Kaminsky is canny enough not to trust the fascists, but foolish enough to have made written contracts with them. That file will save Martin, and quite probably your country too. Take the offer, it is the right time—Martin wouldn't hesitate for a single moment and I urge you to do the same."

More silence while Erika thought about this. I didn't know what to say, I didn't know whether accepting Evelyn's bargain would be the right the thing to do. Could we trust her? Should we put our faith in Dmitri's judgement?

But Erika had already made a decision.

"It's a deal," she said.

DAY 13
Friday
24th June 1994

Berlin: The Volkskammer will today debate Dr. Kaminsky's bill to dissolve the Round Tables. The bill will face a rough passage through parliament after documents were leaked alleging co-operation between Dr. Kaminsky and far-right parties.
Round Tables and Worker's Councils throughout the GDR have responded with calls for mass meetings and demonstrations.
Berlin: Martin Grobe, the suspect in the Krause shooting, has escaped from prison. Grobe's absence was discovered by staff at Rummelsburg prison yesterday morning. The former Republik-schutz officer was on remand for the murder of Hanna Krause, the Chair of the Central Round Table.

08:56
Martin

The hatch in the door clanged open and a guard peered in.

"Back against the wall!" he commanded.

But I stayed on my bed, hands behind my head, listening to the radio. I thought the news of a general strike was far more interesting than anything the guard could offer. But I was wrong.

"Accused 592744, you are being transferred." The guard marched into my cell.

"Why?" I was sitting up now, wondering what they were planning to do with me.

"We can no longer guarantee your safety in this institution. Now get up!"

"Where are you taking me?"

Instead of answering the guard pulled me to my feet and wound choke cuffs around my wrists. He prodded me down the echoing corridors, closed cell doors to either side, barred gate at the end. We were buzzed through the gate and I was taken out of the cell block and into the yard.

Inmates were coming out of the next block and being marched to assembly work in the workshops on the other side of the prison.

"Hey!" I shouted, "I'm Martin Grobe, they're taking-" I didn't get any further because I was on my knees in pain as the guard twisted the cuffs tight around my wrists.

A couple of prisoners saw what was happening, and word spread through the work party. They ignored the warders, moving as one towards me. After that, I was hardly aware of what was happening around me, bile was rising in my throat, fighting with the air that was screaming out of my lungs as the cuffs were twisted tighter. I would have fallen over, but the chain around my wrists was pulling me upright. My stomach heaved and the pain in my wrists eased, I must have vomited and collapsed full length on the concrete because the next thing I knew, another prisoner was helping me sit up. My vision cleared and my hearing returned, a klaxon was wailing, my guard sat on the floor, his own choke cuffs bound his wrists, tying them tight behind his back. Other guards sat close to him, all surrounded by prisoners.

"You're Martin Grobe? They said you'd escaped."

My breathing was heavy and ragged, my wrists burned, pain shot up my arms when I moved my fingers. A part of my brain nagged me to get a grip, to work out what was happening.

I stood up, glad of the hand given by a burly man with a tattooed skull. I looked down at my former guard, he was being held now, kneeling on the floor, two prisoners grasping a shoulder each, waiting for me to kick him, hit him, do whatever I wanted to him.

"Let him go."

The two prisoners shrugged and released the guard.

"We've got this far without spilling blood." My breath was ragged, my words came in spurts. "We shouldn't start now just because the old order is fighting back." The other prisoners were grumbling. "Remember Bautzen? We can do that here, now!"

"Bautzen?"

"We all know what happened in Bautzen prison four years ago, we know how they took over the jail, set up a Prisoners' Council. Isn't it time we did that here?" I looked around at the work party, they were all listening to me, the warders unattended. "Out there, beyond these walls, Kaminsky is trying to destroy the Round Tables and the Workers' Councils. So what better answer than to set up our own Prisoners' Council? This is our first step towards freedom. Who's with me? Let's see some hands!"

There was no need to take hands, the prisoners were ready.

09:01
Karo

As soon as Antje appeared I went to the secretary's office, just as Erika and I had planned.

"Frau *Ministerin* Willehardt asks not to be disturbed."

It was a different secretary from last time, a nicer one who assured me she'd hold all appointments.

That was easier than expected, and satisfied with my success I went back to Antje's office, pausing only to collect the daily papers from a side table.

"I can see the urgency," Antje was telling Erika. "But this goes way beyond my powers-"

"Nobody will question you. Have you seen the newspapers this morning? History is on our side." Erika interrupted.

"I have responsibilities, there's no way I could do this and still carry on as minister. I'd have to resign, all my work ... it would be for nothing."

"This is probably the most important thing you'll ever do. Take a step back—see the bigger picture."

Antje was standing behind her desk, running her fingers through her hair. Erika took the newspapers off me and spread them out before her. Kaminsky's duplicity had made the headlines in all the papers except for the Party's own Neues Deutschland and Junge Welt.

Kaminsky link to fascist murder plot was the Berliner Zeitung's offering, while Die Anderen announced a general strike and called Kaminsky a nazi puppet. In the leader they accused him of complicity in the murder of Hanna Krause: *Dr Kaminsky may not have pulled the trigger, but Hanna's blood still indelibly stains his hands.* It had been a busy night for us, but we'd done our work well. The contents of Evelyn's dossier had been made public, along with the details of the murder of Hanna Krause.

Erika put Katrin's tiny cassette on top of the newspapers. "This is a taped confession by the young fascist who shot Hanna. The case against Martin is crumbling. By releasing him you'll be sending a clear message that Kaminsky is no longer pulling the strings. Releasing Martin gives us all a chance to save the Round Tables."

"You're sure Martin hasn't escaped?"

"Martin's still in custody. And when he walks out of Rummelsburg prison the world will see how the police and prison service have conspired with Kaminsky."

Antje picked up a newspaper and scanned the headlines.

"What's the government here for?" Erika asked her.

"To ensure law and order," Antje replied mechanically, taking another newspaper. "To make the best decisions on behalf of the people."

"Have you forgotten all our years in the *Frauengruppe*, hounded by the Party and the Stasi?" Erika took the newspaper away from Antje, forcing the minister to meet her gaze. "You're here to do the people's will. The will as decided at the grassroots. In April the people voted for devolution of power to community Round Table level. Today the Round Tables are calling for a general strike." Erika held her hand out and I gave her the unsigned order to release Martin. She placed it on the desk, in front of Antje and gave her a pen. "We need you."

I managed to hold myself back until we got out of the Ministry, but when we hit the street I gave Erika a hug.

"We did it!" I shouted.

"Don't yell in my ear!" Erika pulled me away from the entrance and the cop who was stationed there. "Come on, there's still plenty of work to do."

"Don't be such a killjoy, I know we've got work to do, but can't we just be pleased that we're getting somewhere?"

"Let's see how far we get first."

We started walking towards the State Prosecutor's office, the streets around us were empty—it was weird, literally nobody about, just us. It stayed that way until we got to the Opera and cut through to Unter den Linden. Now we could hear shouting, chanting. And sirens. A line of cops wearing helmets and holding shields blocked Marx-Engels-Brücke.

"You got your RS pass with you?" Erika looked nervous.

She already had her pass in her hand. I pulled mine out and the pair of us marched up to the squad commander, showing our passes and demanding to be let through.

"Your funeral," The cop said, shrugging. He wasn't too

concerned about our funeral.

We filtered between the police lines and crossed the bridge onto the island that is home to the seat of the *Volkskammer*, the Palace of the Republic. About ten thousand people were there, most with placards or banners: *No Return to the Dictatorship of the Party!* and *Let The Grassroots Grow!*

The energy in the demo was amazing. Inside the Palace, the *Volkskammer* was sitting, debating whether these people here should be allowed to continue running their own neighbourhoods. The so-called democrats sitting in there were trying to roll back the progress of the last four years. They couldn't be allowed to do that, we wouldn't allow them to do that.

"We have to get a move on, we haven't any time to waste." Erika was pulling me through the crowds by my arm.

I trailed behind her, looking around, feeling inspired by everyone there. Erika had already reached Liebknechtbrücke, the bridge that leads to Alexanderplatz, but her way was barred by a line of riot cops. She held her RS pass out and demanded to be let through, but the cops were doing that no-hear-no-see-no-speak trick they're so good at.

"Constable, I am on State business. Let me through immediately!"

I was directly behind her, but still didn't really see what happened next—the cops sort of shuffled their shields, and all of a sudden Erika was on the floor.

"Fuck's sake! Do you know who this is?" I shouted.

But the cops were back in automaton mode. I pulled Erika out of their reach and helped her up. She had a cut above her eye, I dabbed it with my hankie.

"Listen, you fucking idiots," I was facing up to the cops, "this is Lieutenant Lang of the *Republikschutz*, and you're going to let us through-"

But Erika had hold of my arm, pulling me back. I tried to drag myself out of her grasp and she stumbled. The sudden release made me stagger the other way, just as a truncheon whistled through the space I'd just moved out of. It was so quick I didn't even see which cop was holding it.

I quickly backed up a couple of paces, but now people were pressing in behind us—some demonstrators had seen what was happening and had come to help out. They had their arms linked and were chanting *Keine Gewalt!*—no violence.

Erika stood facing the protestors, her arms outstretched.

"It's OK, it's OK. We're here to show the *Volkskammer* that they can't ignore us, so let's do that, let's go back to the main entrance of the Palace of the Republic!"

It did the job, our new friends ebbed away, leaving space in front of the police lines. Erika took my arm and pulled me with her. This time I let her.

We went back to Marx-Engels-Brücke, the way we'd come in, but when we got there the officer that had let us in was nowhere to be seen. Erika didn't hesitate though, she just pulled out her RS pass again, holding it at arm's length and marching towards the ranked cops. I saw the shields move sideways, making a gap just in front of Erika and I grabbed her shoulder, jerking her backwards just as the cop in front lifted his arm, truncheon ready to hammer down.

We stumbled back into the crowd, I was still holding onto Erika.

"You OK?" she asked me.

"Am I OK? You're asking if I'm OK? You nearly got your head split open—Erika, you're even harder than I thought!"

But Erika was already trying to find a way through the crowd. "We have to get through, let's try the Rathausbrücke on the other side of the Palace of the Republic."

"We can't go! These cops are just waiting to kick off!"

The crowd was getting restless, shouts chorused up and down the square, some pissed up idiots were taunting the line of cops behind us.

"Karo, you stay if you think it's important. I'm going to get Martin's release order to the State Prosecutor, we haven't got any time to waste and Martin's my priority."

Shit, she was right. I felt dead bad about leaving the demo, solidarity and all, but this time we had a different mission.

We pushed past the Palace of the Republic, down to the other end of Marx-Engels-Platz. But our way was blocked by yet another line of cops, keeping us kettled in front of the Palace.

"Do you reckon they'll let us through this time?" Erika asked, but the answer was obvious.

"There's less of them here," I said. "They're not so close together. If I create a diversion you might be able to run through one of the gaps."

At least it was a plan. Sometimes it worked, mostly it didn't, and when it didn't whoever was trying to jump through the police lines got a good kicking. But I couldn't think of anything else to do, apart from trying to mobilise the demonstration—and that was just a recipe for cracked heads and broken ribs.

"We can try to get into the Palace, then we can make some calls, get someone to fetch us out of here."

"Erika, that plan's as shit as mine. They're not letting anyone inside—didn't you see the cops barricading the foyer?"

Erika was facing the cops, she was thinking, her eyes taking in the gaps in the line, how they widened and narrowed as the bulls shifted nervously from foot to foot.

"I'll get a few people here to help," she said eventually. "We'll do the diversion thing and you can jump through. You can run faster than me, you've got a much better chance."

But it was already too late: three olive-green lorries were driving on to the bridge in front of us. Men wearing fatigues were jumping out of the back.

"Here come reinforcements," muttered Erika.

Martin

When I tried to walk my legs collapsed under me. I was
helped up again, and I staggered over to the boiler house
where the prisoners were gathering. Some had gone off to
release those still locked in their cells, and the warders were
being ushered out of the main gate. A couple of men had
climbed the water tower and were hanging a bedsheet
daubed with boot polish: *Under New Management.*

It wasn't long before I was surrounded by hundreds. We
sat in groups with others from our cell blocks, and within a
few minutes spokes from each block had been selected and
were sitting in the middle, putting together a list of what we
needed to talk about and what we needed to do.

It wasn't long before they asked me to speak.

"My name is Martin Grobe, you may have heard of me.
Perhaps you saw me in the newspapers last year, or heard
about me on the radio. I helped to stop a plot by ex-Stasi
officers. And I was there a few weeks ago when the
population of our country united to stand against skinhead
thugs and fascists. I'm on remand for the murder of Hanna
Krause. If any of you are in any doubt, let me tell you this: I
did not shoot her."

"We're all innocent here!" some wit shouted to applause
and laughter.

"Hanna was my friend." The chuckling died out. "I knew
and worked with her for years. I can't say the same about
Kaminsky—he stands for everything I never want to see
again. But even if I'd had a gun in my hand last Saturday,
even if I'd had the opportunity, I wouldn't have killed him.
Kaminsky and the Party need a way to make us afraid,
they're trying to make us want the security that they're
promising. I'm here because they need a scapegoat. I'm here
so they can point to me and say: *You can't trust anyone!*"

There were mumbles of agreement coming from the

prisoners around me, I waited until I had their attention again.

"Remember Lenin? *Trust is good, control is better.* Today the country decides whether we want control or trust. Today the country decides: representative democracy controlled by the elite and the politicians; or grassroots democracy working through Round Tables and Councils just like the one we're starting here?

"Out there, the country is on general strike. Out there, the people—not Kaminsky's People—but the people of the GDR, the people who live and work and play in the GDR, the people who came here from other places and the people who were born here—they are all deciding for themselves whether they want the Party back, or whether they want to carry on this experiment that we started in 1989.

"It's time for us to choose, too. Are we with them? Are we with the people of the GDR? Are we on strike?"

09:42

Karo

The men in fatigues fell into columns and rapidly marched over the bridge to relieve the regular police units. It was scary how efficient they were; it took less than a minute to replace the lines. The cops were initially a bit unsure what to do, but a non-com took them in hand and marched them off towards Alexanderplatz.

"You notice anything?" Erika asked.

Only a million things, like how scary those lads looked. How fucking confident and efficient they were.

"Look," Erika insisted, like I wasn't already looking. "They're not carrying shields, they're not armed: no guns, not even truncheons."

Shit, how had I *not* noticed that? What I did notice, though, was one of the trucks moving over the bridge. The line of uniforms opened to let it drive through.

"And, look at their epaulettes. The corps colours."

I didn't know what corps colours were, and anyway, I had my eyes glued to that truck. The hatch in the roof of the cab was opening.

"That isn't the *Volkspolizei*, that's-"

"It's Rico!"

Rico the border guard had stood up in the hatch, megaphone in hand.

"*Achtung! Achtung!* This is *not* the police. I repeat, this is *not the police.*" The amplified sound of Rico's voice bounced off the Palace, sending shock waves through the demonstration. Everyone was looking at Rico, daunted at the sight of army trucks at the demo. "Do not be alarmed. We are here to guarantee your democratic rights. We have relieved the police of their duties and you are free to stay or to leave as you choose. I repeat: you are free to stay, or to leave."

A file of border guards was now making its way through the crowd, heading for the entrance to the Palace of the Republic.

"Please allow my comrades through. They are going to the Palace of the Republic to enable an orderly and safe withdrawal of police forces."

"They've got nothing to fear from us!" someone shouted.

But Rico didn't answer, because I was scrambling up into the cab of his truck.

"Is this a mutiny?" I asked as I squeezed past him through the hatch.

Climbing onto the roof of the cab I gave Rico a hug, and the crowd yelled its approval, then I took the megaphone.

"*Kaminsky out! Wir sind das Volk!*" I shouted.

The crowd shouted right back, so loud I had to put my hands over my ears. I was just raising the megaphone to my lips again when I saw Erika below, hands on her hips, doing a Laura face.

"Karo, come down here this instant!"

I laughed at her, and Erika's face lifted into a smile. I slid down off the roof, Rico holding my arms as I hung over the windscreen. I landed on the ground, and had to push my way through the crowd gathering around the truck, cheering and hugging the border guards. By the time I got to Erika, she was talking to Rico. He was listening carefully, finger crooked below his lip.

"Get into the back of the truck, we'll take you—you won't make it by yourself. Public transport is on strike, the police have set up checkpoints. There are marches and demos all over Berlin."

Rico got into the cab and we clambered into the back along with a few border guards.

It took only a few minutes to get to the Court on Littenstrasse, and Erika climbed over the tailgate to go into the building. Rico came into the back of the truck and talked for a bit to the radio operator. I sat and waited, listening to the noises and chants of another demonstration, just round the corner on Alexanderplatz.

A few minutes later Erika reappeared.

"Got it!" She handed me an envelope before clambering up into the back of the truck.

I opened the envelope and looked at the letter from the General State Prosecutor.

"Have you seen how many stamps are on this piece of paper?" I asked Erika.

"Five," she answered, and looked like she was going to tell me what they all were and why they were there.

But I'd stopped listening, I was about to burst with excitement—I was on the back of an army truck (no, make that a mutineering army truck) and I was holding the piece of paper that would get Martin out of the clink.

And once Martin was out of jail we'd sort Kaminsky and his shitty plans.

Martin

They wanted to elect me as a representative, but I said no. Some weren't very happy about that and started arguing with me.

"If you want a figurehead then I'm the wrong one to choose. Not interested. The only ones interested in that kind of thing are people like Kaminsky."

It was the wrong thing to say, and the spokescouncil descended into arguments, but finally things began to settle down, and more immediate issues were considered.

"We need to get ourselves sorted," a grey haired prisoner said. "Any moment now the screws are going to come in here looking for revenge."

But it was already too late: one of the lookouts up the water tower was pointing towards the front gate. "Screws on the march!"

I'd found my feet again and was able to follow everyone else around the corner to see what was happening.

A squad of warders, wearing helmets, carrying shields and truncheons, had come through the steel door at the entrance and were waiting to go through the first of two gates in the wire fence. Their visors were down, it was hard to see their faces, but you could tell that they were spoiling for a fight.

A buzzer sounded, and the first gate slid open.

The warders marched up to the second gate, drumming truncheons on shields as they came.

Karo

A police checkpoint blocked the main road near the Hauptbahnhof, so we turned left, heading into Friedrichshain. It was so eerie, the streets were completely empty—apart from the cops we hadn't seen a soul since Alexanderplatz. But that all changed as we turned off at

Franz-Mehring-Platz. If the empty streets had been weird, then this was even weirder. Sitting on the grass, on kitchen chairs or standing around, everyone was facing the middle of the square where several people were having some kind of discussion. More people were leaning over the balconies of the tower blocks surrounding the square. Before I could make anything else out we'd swung around the corner and the Neues Deutschland printing works blocked the view.

"That was unexpected," I said to Erika, but she was lost in her own thoughts.

We crossed Warschauer Strasse—normally full of bikes, people, shoppers—now it was just empty. But when Boxhagener Platz hove into view we could see another gathering—hundreds of people sitting there while five or six figures stood in the middle discussing. As I watched, an old lady got off her chair, went to one of the standing figures, tapped her on the shoulder and then took her place. The woman who had been talking went and sat down.

The truck ground on, and as we drew near to the RS offices Rico rapped on the back window of the cab, and held up four fingers.

One of border guards put a clunky pair of headphones on and leaned over the radio, playing around with it for a moment or two.

"Berta zwo Berta zwo Berta zwo. This is Anton eins, over."

The radio crackled a bit, then: "Berta zwo receiving, over."

"Anton eins, execute orders zero-four, over."

"Berta zwo, zero four received, out."

A couple of minutes after the cryptic message we were passing under the railway bridges near Rummelsburg station when I saw another olive-green truck coming from the right.

"Hey guys, are they on our side?"

Instead of answering, the sparky pushed the tarp further back and waved. The truck behind us flashed its headlights, and the hatch in its cab roof clanged open. A dude in a

Hawaiian shirt popped up, heaving a massive camera onto his shoulder. He was pointing it in our direction.

"What the fuck?"

"West TV, they've come to join the fun." The sparky smiled.

"But the border's closed!"

"We brought them over on a customs launch. They climbed out of a window in Kreuzberg, a customs boat was waiting for them on the river below."

OK, this was a bit much. Here was this platoon or regiment or whatever it was, just turning up and turfing out the cops, and now the customs boats and stuff. What was going on?

"Did Rico organise all of this? Are you all, like, under his command or something?"

The border guards in the back of the truck with us had a laugh about that, and Erika began to pay attention.

"The Soldiers' Council of the Border Regiment 33 had a meeting this morning. We're on strike."

"You call this being on strike?"

"Yeah, fun isn't it?"

Fuck me, I think this classed as another revolution!

We pulled up in front of the prison, and Erika climbed out. She stalked over to the sentry, looking dead imposing. I scrambled down after her, but the guy in the Hawaiian shirt and his camera beat me to it. He shoved the camera right into the sentry's face and the poor git had Erika on one side and this massive camera on the other. He didn't know what to do. He lifted the telephone and made his report: *There are representatives from the General State Prosecutor's office here.*

We went through the big steel door, into that scary bit by the administration building—high gates blocking the way forward and back, a sentry box and a watchtower spying on us. Shouting could be heard from inside the prison, even louder than the noise demo the other day. Erika was already half way up the front steps of the admin block, and I was about to run after her when I heard someone shouting my name.

"Karo! Karo, wait!"

It was weird, my mind must have been addled—too much sun or excitement or something—I could swear it was Katrin's voice. Hawaiian-shirt dude and his sound crew were trying to manoeuvre all their tat through the gate, and squeezing through the middle of them all was Katrin.

She ran up and hugged me. I nearly dissolved into a puddle, but I took a step back before I lost it.

"Karo, I've got an apology to make-"

"What the fuck are you doing here? Listen, Katrin, not a good time, really not-"

"I know, I know, I came with the TV crew. Now go—go and do what you need to do—I'll be here, waiting for you."

I hesitated for a moment, not knowing whether to hug her or apologise or just walk way.

I turned to look for Erika, but she was already out of sight, so I decided to go up the watchtower, see what was happening on the other side of the prison walls. I climbed up the ladder, the TV crew just behind me. The three wardens at the top tried to bar my way when they saw me coming up.

"Stand aside, I'm from the General State Prosecutor's office!" I waved my RS pass at them, making sure to move it around enough so they couldn't get a good look.

Looking out of the window I couldn't believe my eyes—it was a full scale revolt down there! A load of tooled up wardens were trying to get through the last fence, they looked like they were ready for business. Prisoners were trying to chain the gate shut, but the bastard screws were ramming truncheons through the fence to stop them.

"Call the guards back, tell them to fall back!" I ordered the nearest screw.

He hesitated, looking down at what was happening below, then at me, then at the TV camera.

"I'm only going to say this once more, and if you don't do it then I will make sure the General State Prosecutor herself hears about this."

The guard's finger moved towards a switch, he pressed it and leaned over the microphone: "Tactical Unit stand down. Tactical Unit stand down."

Wow! I couldn't believe I just made that happen! I could definitely get used to ordering people around. I watched as the riot-screws dribbled away from the inner compound— they looked really pissed off, even I could tell that might be a problem. I went to the window on the other side of the tower, the side that looked down on the space outside the admin block, and shoved it open.

"Rico, you need to get up here!"

Back at the control panel. I pressed the switch and bent over the mike: "This is Round Table Task Force One," I made that bit up but it sounded good—all the prisoners were cheering and waving. "Is Martin Grobe with you? We're looking for Martin Grobe."

The mass of uniformed prisoners was moving, someone was being pushed towards the front, and there he was: Martin, looking up at the tower. He had his hands cupped in front of his mouth and was shouting something, but no way could I hear anything through all that cheering.

I pressed the button again. "Martin, wait there, don't go anywhere!"

Rico had reached us now, so I asked him to send a couple of his men up, "Make sure these clowns don't try anything stupid."

Rico did some hand signals through the window and all of a sudden there were too many people in the tower. Rico and I went back down the ladder, taking the TV crew with us.

I told Rico I was worried about the screws in the yard,

they were psyched up, ready to fight and we needed to make sure we outnumbered them. "Can you get more of your colleagues?"

Rico shook his head. "It'll take at least twenty minutes, maybe thirty." He headed over to the lorry where the sparky was fiddling with his radio, and I looked around for Katrin. She was being interviewed by the telly people, but I dragged her away from them.

"Katrin, your dad's OK, I've just seen him. We're going to get him out of there any moment now."

Katrin was fighting back tears, and I was welling up too, but I couldn't afford to lose it, not today, not now.

I was saved by Rico.

"There'll be forty men here soon."

"No guns?"

"No guns." He confirmed.

I looked around the yard, there was too much going on, a DDR TV crew had turned up and were filming as well, some screws were standing around, unsure what to do. The outer gate was still open, and when I peered through the gap I could see a police patrol car outside. Leaning on the door, smoking, was Steinlein. He took the ciggie out of his mouth and gave me a smile, like he was happy to see his best mate. I ignored him, wishing he would go away.

But something was nagging at the back of my head, I was missing something: Erika.

I looked at my watch, and wondered what was taking her so long. She'd been in the admin block for at least ten minutes, and that made me jumpy. I grabbed a couple of Rico's border guards and went up the steps. We were just about to go through the doors when a buzzer sounded. Looking over my shoulder I could see the inner gate opening, tooled up screws were streaming through.

I watched them march through the gate, not able to move,

not able to make the decision: grab Katrin and leg it out the main gate, away from these scary, radge fuckers; or try to find Erika, make sure she succeeded in getting Martin free.

"Katrin! Get out! Go now, go!" I screamed over my shoulder as I ran up the steps into the admin block. Up the stairs to the first floor, but more screws were coming the other way, a couple tried to grab me, but the border guards overtook me, batting the screws down the stairs. More wardens were clattering up behind us.

"Hold them off—long as you can!" I shouted above the sound of the klaxon.

I could hear yells and scuffling as I ran up the last few steps, I charged down the corridor and shouldered open the door to the director's office.

"Call your men off!" I shouted into the room.

"As I was explaining to Lieutenant Lang," the director ignored my demand—the supercilious bastard didn't even bother looking at me—"releasing a prisoner is out of the question at the present time. As you can see the whole institution is in lockdown-"

"Listen, Mr. Director." I leaned over his desk, putting my face in front of his. "First of all you're going to get your men to stop being macho idiots. Then you're going to hand over Martin Grobe. I don't care whether you're in lockdown or in fucking meltdown!"

"I think it's time you left. Comrade Lieutenant, perhaps you could take your young colleague with you?"

"We're not going until we've got Martin!" I was shouting at him now. I really, really wanted to punch the arrogant shit.

In fact, I might have punched him, but I was distracted by another voice: calm, pedantic, infuriating, "Thank you, Frau Rengold."

It was Steinlein. He must have followed us up here. I was about to tell him to mind his own business when he addressed the director.

"It's time to let Grobe go, Director. You may phone Captain Neumann if you wish to confirm the order."

Suddenly it was a completely different guy behind the desk, he'd turned into an obsequious shit.

"Certainly, comrade Lieutenant. One moment." He was already reaching for the phone, ready to pass on the order to release Martin.

Erika was ushering me towards the door. As we passed Steinlein she gave him a long, hard look.

Martin showed his wrists to the TV crew, and they zoomed in on the bracelets of livid contusions. Gross. After all the hugs and excitement we stood around, wondering what the hell to do next. We'd been concentrating so much on getting Martin out of the prison that we hadn't really had a chance to plan any further.

We withdrew to the edge of the road in front of the prison where Rico marshalled his men onto the trucks and the telly crews were trying to persuade the prison guards to give interviews.

Steinlein was back by his squad car, smoking, when Martin shook his hand. "I hear your bluff was what got me out?"

"Might be wise not to stay here too long—they may still change their minds."

We piled into the back of one of Rico's trucks and headed towards Friedrichshain, Steinlein following in his police car. Martin was at the end of the bench with Katrin next to him. I sat on the other side of her, our hands sort of touching. She didn't pull away, and nor did I. In fact, her fingers closed around mine and I squeezed back. My heart was beating so fast it felt like I was going to pop.

Ten minutes later we were at Boxhagener Platz. We helped Martin down from the back of the truck and sat at the edge of the big group of people we'd driven past earlier.

There must have been a few thousand people there, and despite the PA we could hardly make out what was being said. Every so often one of the speakers was replaced by another person who'd been waiting.

"What's going on?" Martin asked someone sitting on the grass nearby.

"Neighbourhood Round Table. We had to hold it in the square because so many people wanted to participate. Kaminsky's plans have backfired, the Round Tables are more popular than ever—there are mass meetings being held all over the country!"

The guy's enthusiasm was all a bit too much for me and I wandered off, leaving Martin to natter with his new friend. Steinlein sat in his cop car, making everyone feel uncomfortable just by being there and Erika had disappeared into the crowd, I could see her chatting with someone. I wanted a moment for myself—too much had happened and I needed a chance to catch up.

Katrin saw me move away and jumped up to run after me. We stood facing each other, just a few centimetres apart, neither of us sure what to say.

"I'm glad you came," I managed after a bit.

Katrin just nodded, her eyes not quite meeting mine.

"Well, this is awkward ..." I went for humorous, but it didn't work.

In fact things just got even more awkward because Schimmel bounced up. I hadn't seen him this happy for yonks, and most of me smiled to see him like this, but a big part of me just wanted him to go away and leave me and Katrin to our scary, stiff non-conversation. Didn't he have any tact? Couldn't he see Katrin and I were trying to talk?

"Come on you two! This is amazing, this is the best day ever! You got Martin out!"

"It's just the start—we're not even halfway there yet."

"You're having me on?" Schimmel stopped his bouncing

218

and examined Katrin and me. "No, you've really not heard, have you? The Volkskammer voted against Kaminsky!" Schimmel's mouth widened into a smile. "And guess what? *Neues Forum* reintroduced the bill to devolve power to the Round Tables—the other parties were so scared of being tarred with the same brush as Kaminsky that they just nodded it through—the Round Tables are here to stay!"

"You're kidding? Really—we won?" I was jumping up and down, this was it, we'd done it, we'd seen off Kaminsky!

Schimmel and I grabbed Katrin, and it all turned into a group hug. I felt like shouting, like running around and setting off fireworks.

"I missed you." Katrin's voice was muffled, her head pressed against mine.

I let go of Schimmel, and he must have had more tact than I'd given him credit for because he went over to Martin. It was just Katrin and me—the whole of Boxhagener Platz, the whole of Friedrichshain had faded away. I had my hands on Katrin's shoulders, she was looking at the ground.

"I know it's not cool to say that I missed you, but I did," she mumbled.

I was hastily wiping tears away with the back of my hand.

"Can I have a hug?" She looked up, her face red.

I put my arms around her, not saying a word, just burying myself in her hair.

"If I come home, will you be willing to give it a go? I mean, give me a go?" Katrin asked, her lips tickling my ear.

"Home? Here?" I moved my head back so I could see her. It was all that I wanted, but it was too much to take in.

"It's time to come back to East Berlin. You're right, there so much work to do, I want to do it with you. Will you ... can we do that? Can you give me-"

I hugged Katrin, hard. With all my strength I pulled her into me. My tears wet her hair.

Martin

It was such a relief, a relief to allow myself to feel optimistic again, to feel that we might be getting somewhere. The people here on Boxhagener Platz were really involved in their local Round Table, they were participating, *owning* it. For years I'd been waiting for this, hoping for this, but instead I'd watched the chances for our participatory democracy dwindle as people struggled to survive the everyday battles of their lives, leaving decisions to the career politicians.

But here they were, brought together to save something that was on the verge of dissolution. And not just here, but everywhere in the country.

Katrin and Karo were off to one side, hugging each other and looking happy. Schimmel was giving me a detailed account of the proceedings in the *Volkskammer* this morning. I was glad to have them all with me—they were excited, proud even—I could feel the enthusiasm coming off them. Enthusiasm was a good thing to have—after all, it was going to be up to them and their generation to shape our country.

My deliberations were interrupted by a hand on my shoulder. It was Steinlein.

"I've been monitoring the radio—there's a police squad coming to arrest you," he said, his hand gripping my shoulder painfully.

"Here? How do they know I'm here?"

"We need to go, come on. I'll take you somewhere safe."

"I have to let Katrin know-"

"No time, come on, we have to go, right now!" Steinlein still had hold of my shoulder and was pulling me towards his police car.

"Schimmel—tell Katrin!" I shouted as Steinlein pushed me into the passenger seat.

"I'm going to put these on you." He held a pair of

handcuffs. "If we're stopped then I can say I'm taking you in. OK?"

I nodded, my mind numb, working too slowly to keep up with events. The cuffs clicked around my wrists and Steinlein put the Lada into gear.

"I'll take you to my allotment, once we're there we can work out what to do next."

I nodded again, not really taking in what Steinlein was saying. He twisted the volume knob on the police radio, listening to the staccato messages as he drove the car south. We went over the river and passed under the S-Bahn tracks near Baumschulenweg station, a few minutes after that we pulled up outside an allotment colony.

I got out to open the gate, feeling awkward with my cuffed hands, and Steinlein drove through, parking a few metres down the sandy track.

When I caught up with him, the policeman was still sitting in the driver's seat, his eyes red-rimmed, hands on the steering wheel, arms stiff. The radio was chattering, static almost drowning out the words.

"Somebody saw us," he told the windscreen. "They've put out an alert for both of us, we have to change vehicles."

Steinlein jerked into action, sliding out of the police car and looking around the lane. A Trabant was parked a few metres away, bright sunlight glaring off the windscreen. Steinlein tried the passenger door, it was unlocked. He held it open for me to get in.

I hesitated, threads of doubt beginning to unfurl down my spine.

"Get in!" Steinlein ordered, practically shoving me into the car. He slapped the door shut and swung around to the driver's side, pulling off his cap and uniform blouson as he went.

I tried to grab the door handle, wanting to get back out, but my manacled hands were making me clumsy

"I wouldn't do that if I were you." It wasn't Steinlein, it was another voice, one I knew well. Smooth, but dangerous, a shiv dipped in honey. My spine seized under the pressure of a gun barrel.

"Evelyn."

"Clever boy. Couldn't go without saying goodbye, could I?" Evelyn replied.

Steinlein had got the Trabant started, and the engine howled as we pulled out of the allotments and onto the road.

"What do you mean, goodbye?"

"Time to go. You're my ticket out of here, dear heart."

Ignoring the dead metal of the gun I twisted around, trying to catch sight of my nemesis in the back seat.

"My work here is done, and I couldn't have done it without you—you've been an immense help." She laughed at my blank face. "We needed to get rid of Kaminsky."

"You knew about the plot? You set me up?"

"Sorry, my dear. If there'd been any other way ... As it is, Lieutenant Steinlein here was our agent—we knew of Kaminsky's every move. But I do hope your brief stay in jail wasn't *too* horrendous."

"You should have left me there."

"Now, now, don't be bitter. Don't forget, you also wanted to get rid of Kaminsky. Now we've assigned that populist dreck to the dustbin of history the Party can get on with the real job of sorting out the mess your counter-revolution is causing. Kaminsky was just the warm up act, now it's time for the Party to really start its comeback."

"Fuck you!"

Steinlein wasn't participating in the pleasantries, he was concentrating on the road, hammering the Trabant.

"Oh, and if you get the chance, please do thank your colleagues for the small but significant roles they played."

"My colleagues?"

"Oh wake up, dear Martin. Yes, the amateur spies from RS,

not to forget that bumptious fool, Dmitri Alexandrovich. Couldn't have done it without them, although I suspect they won't be too pleased when they hear that. I spun them a little line, told them I wanted to stay here. They seemed to trust me after that, the darlings."

The engine screeched as Steinlein shifted gear and with a vicious yank of the wheel we turned into Sonnenallee. I was thrown against the door as the car skeetered around the corner, another howl of the engine as Steinlein stamped on the accelerator. The little Trabant was galloping towards the border crossing, the guard barracks and the tall spotlights loomed larger as we careered up the road.

"The border?"

"Do *try* to keep up darling, I've already told you—you're my ticket out of here."

"Don't say a fucking word," Steinlein muttered as a border guard waved us to a halt.

"Papers please." The guard saluted.

Evelyn's gun had slipped down from my neck, now pressing into my left side, Steinlein's body hiding it from anyone outside the car. Steinlein himself hadn't reacted, he was still hunched over the steering wheel, revving the engine and peering through the dirty windscreen.

Evelyn reached forward and passed her papers through the driver's open window. The guard checked the *Ausweis*, took a closer look at Evelyn and stepped back, his eyes widening in surprise.

"Yes sweetheart, I'm Evelyn Hagenow, and I'm on your most-wanted list. But you're going to let us through, and you're going to radio your comrades to tell them not to stop us." Evelyn moved the gun forwards, allowing the guard to see it. "Because if we aren't allowed into West Berlin then comrade Captain Martin Grobe here, national treasure that he is, will have made his final journey."

Steinlein lifted his foot off the clutch, and the car jumped forward, curving through the gateway in the first wall, tyres slipping on the cracked concrete.

The second wall of the checkpoint was looming, the gap looked impossibly narrow.

"Stop! Let me out!" I was panicking, my chained hands struggling to find the door handle.

We slalomed around bollards, through the next wall, my hands were braced against the dashboard. I could no longer feel the gun barrel pressing into my body, Evelyn needed both hands to hang on. Steinlein shifted down two gears, the engine screamed and the wheels left the road as the Trabant bucked through the narrow gap. Another wall bore down on us, just metres ahead, Steinlein heaved the steering wheel to the right, his shoulder jutting into mine as he forced the car around. His knee went down as his foot slammed onto the accelerator again, through another gap, around chicanes. The last wall was before us, a border guard jumped out of the way as the car lined up for the final opening. Another few metres and we'd be in West Berlin.

Giving up on the door handle, I pulled my fingers into fists and slammed the metal handcuffs into Steinlein's wrist, knocking his hand off the steering wheel. Grabbing the wheel, I dragged it towards me, sending the car off to the right. The wheels bumped over a curb, a wing crumpled against a bollard and the Trabant rebounded, two wheels no longer in contact with the road. We hung there for an eternity, breath held, Steinlein meeting my eyes, his hate melding our fates together.

The car glissaded back to earth, spinning into the concrete wall. The windscreen crazed into opacity, the engine died.

"You'll never win." My voice was as pitted as the windscreen, my neck tense, expecting a bullet. "You may try to escape, you may try to stop us." Border guards surrounded the car, each levelling a machine pistol. Steinlein's door was torn open, rough hands grabbed him, pulling him out, other hands plucked Evelyn from the back seat. "We are the people, the people of the GDR, with all our dreams and hopes and convictions. With all our colours and histories and cultures."

But there was nobody to hear me, Steinlein and Evelyn had been taken away.

"We are the people, and we will always win," I said, wondering who I was trying to persuade.

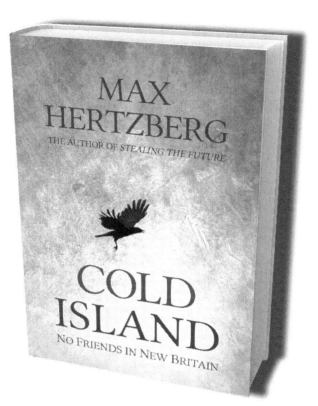

COLD ISLAND

It's more than twenty-five years since Mara arrived in Britain, yet today she no longer feels safe in the country she thought she knew.

When threatened with deportation, Mara goes underground and meets others who have made their home in the UK but are now leading lives in the half-shadows of society.

Hoping to reach relative safety in Scotland, they embark on a journey across the moors of northern England—but Immigration Enforcement is never far behind.

A portrayal of Britain looking into the abyss of nationalism and xenophobia.

Printed in Great Britain
by Amazon

38144963R00139